Strictly Business

IONA ROSE

Author's Note

Hey there!

Thank you for choosing my book. I sure hope that you love it. I'd hate to part ways once you're done though. So how about we stay in touch?

My newsletter is a great way to discover more about me and my books. Where you'll find frequent exclusive giveaways, sneak previews of new releases and be first to see new cover reveals.

And as a HUGE thank you for joining, you'll receive a FREE book on me!

With love,

Iona

Get Your FREE Book Here:
https://dl.bookfunnel.com/v9yit8b3f7

Publisher: SomeBooks

Strictly Business
Copyright © 2023 Iona Rose
The right of Iona Rose to be identified as the Author of the Work has been
asserted by her in accordance with the copyright, designs and patent act
1988.

CHAPTER 1

Wyatt

I look at my watch and I'm surprised to note it's almost nine pm. The surprise is not because I'm still in the office – that's normal for me and it would be more of a surprise if I was home at this time. I am surprised because I thought it was much earlier than it is. Apparently, time flies when you're swamped with work, not just when you are having fun, although the two are often interchangeable for me as I genuinely love my job.

Ignoring the thought of dinner, I get back into work mode and I open the next email to be dealt with. It's simple enough. One of my graphic designers has sent a campaign to be finalized. I look over the designs. Overall, they are good, and I like them a lot, but I do have a few small tweaks that need completing. I note these down and send the new file back to the designer. The tweaks are small enough that some people would say that I was nit-picking, but I'm a perfectionist and my team knows that. I think they would be more concerned if I signed off on a campaign immediately than when I take the time to look over it and help them to strengthen it.

I'm about to open the next email in my inbox when my

cell phone rings. The ring pierces the soft silence that has settled around me. I look around my desk, searching for my ringing cell phone, but it isn't there. It must be close because I can hear it trilling, the sound seeming to get angrier the longer I ignore it. I realize the sound is coming from the top drawer of my desk. I pull it open and take my cell phone out.

"Wyatt McAvoy," I mutter, as I swipe the screen.

"Craig West," an amused voice say. He laughs, then starts taking the piss out of me. "Wyatt McAvoy. What the hell, man? What happened to, yeah what's up?"

I grin at the sound of his warm gruff voice. "I couldn't find my cell phone and by the time I did, I figured it was almost ready to stop ringing so I just swiped quickly without looking at the screen," I say. "Now what could I have possibly done to deserve this pleasure?"

Craig is my best friend and has been since we started high school. We went through high school and then college together and even now, in our early forties, we are still close, so I find it a bit strange when Craig sounds awkward when he next speaks.

"Actually, I wanted to ask you for a favor," he says.

We regularly roped each other into doing things like helping each other move apartments or decorate rooms before we were making enough money to pay other people to do stuff like that. And even now, if either of us needs anything, we go to each other first. Which is why I find it odd that Craig sounds so awkward all of a sudden. It's not like this is unprecedented territory for us.

I wonder if he needs to borrow some money.

Of course, I'd be happy to lend him whatever he needs, but that's one scenario I never thought I'd see Craig in...ever.

"Go on," I say when it seems like Craig isn't going to say anything without me prompting him to speak up.

He sighs and I picture him getting his courage up. I'm starting to feel a bit nervous now. What can he possibly want from me that he's this reluctant to ask for? I sense it's about something more than just money.

"Could you possibly give Serena a job?" Craig finally says.

Serena is Craig's niece. I remember her well enough from before she went off to college. She was a plump little thing with a mass of mousey brown curls that were always in disarray, and she wore horrible wire framed glasses that were too big for her face, making her eyes look strangely bug like. But she was a sweet girl and she had always been polite to me. Considering she'd gotten into an ivy league college she must be intelligent too.

None of that mattered though. I had to say no, and Craig knew it. I felt bad to say no to him, especially after how awkward he had been about asking, but he too understood the score. He was awkward about asking because he knew I was going to have to say no.

"I'm sorry man. You know I love you, but you also know my number one rule of business – never mix business and pleasure, or in this case, friendship."

"I get that," Craig said, suddenly more confident. "But this isn't you taking on a dud as a favor to me. It would be you taking on a great asset as a favor to yourself. I've seen some of her work Wyatt and she's good. Real good. And don't forget she's got a degree in business management and marketing from Harvard. In fact, the more I think about it, the more I think I am actually doing you a favor asking you to have Serena go and work for you."

I knew she had gone ivy league, but I had no idea where and I certainly hadn't known that her degree was actually relevant to what she would be doing here if I was to give her a job. My company, Smart Marketing Solutions, is, as the name suggests, a marketing firm. We take care of a company's branding and message, and we design ads for various social media platforms, ads for old school media like newspapers and magazines, and TV ads. We also have a team working on viral content for platforms such as Instagram and TikTok.

And I do need a new associate.

Since I just promoted my last associate to marketing executive which means she's off in the company on her own now working on her own portfolio. I need an associate to help with my workload because I have to run the company as well as take care of my personal clients. Could I take a chance on Serena? If there was anyone I would be willing to break my rule for it would be Craig, or his brother, Martin, Serena's father.

"If I did agree to employ her, and I'm not yet, I'm just talking hypothetically, she wouldn't get any special treatment. She would be treated like any other associate which is the bottom rung of the ladder," I say.

"Of course, I get that, and she does too," Craig says immediately. "She's not looking for any special treatment, she just wants someone to give her a fair chance. You remember what it was like leaving college with your degree and realizing it was next to impossible to get a foot in the door anywhere decent."

I do remember it. I remember it well. It was that struggle to find anything worth doing, which eventually led me to start my own firm. It seemed that was the only way in without knowing someone in the industry because the positions I saw advertised where always for someone with years of experience, something I couldn't get because no one would give me a chance.

"I know you're a bit reluctant to give her a chance because you know her," Craig adds into the silence. "But I guarantee, if she turned up for an associate position interview with that degree and her portfolio and you had no idea who she was, you'd be begging her to take the position."

I know he's probably right, and I can feel myself relenting. I suppose Craig is right in a way. It's as wrong to overlook someone just because you know them as it is to employ them purely because you know them.

"If I did take her on, you'd have to promise not to interfere and you would need to understand that if it's not working out, I won't hesitate to get rid of her, just like I would anyone else," I say. "And you would need to make sure Martin understands the same thing."

"I know," Craig replies. "But she won't let you down. I know she won't."

"Fine," I say with a sigh. "Tell her to be here at nine o'clock sharp Monday morning."

"Thanks Wyatt, you're the man," Craig says happily.

"Make sure she understands this though – knowing the right person got her in the door, but only performing in her role will keep her on this side of it," I say.

"Got it. Thanks again. Catch you later man," Craig says.

He ends the call before I can speak, probably to make sure I can't change my mind. Should I change my mind? Probably, but I won't. I've said I'll give Serena a chance and I will, and I just have to trust that Craig is mature enough to not sever our friendship if Serena working here doesn't work out.

CHAPTER 2

Wyatt

Monday Morning
Nine o'clock sharp

I take a sip of my hot then quickly scan over my schedule for the day. The next hour or so is the only time I have to return emails and phone calls because my day is completely full of meetings from around eleven o'clock. I could move a meeting or two if I have to, but I'm hoping that won't be the case because truth be told, I'd like to get these meetings done and out of the way. I put my hand on the receiver of my phone, ready to pick it up and call one of my clients, when there is a knock on my door. It can only be Ruth, my personal assistant.

"Come in," I call.

I look up as the door opens. Ruth is tall and very thin, to my mind to the point of being scrawny, but she considers herself to be fashionably slim. I can see the bones at the top of her chest in the skintight black dress she's wearing. The blunt bob she wears her sleek black hair in hangs close to her jaw, showing off her best feature, a swan-line graceful neck. I guess she wouldn't look out of place in the offices of Vogue.

"What's up?"

"It's kind of a strange one," she says. "There's a young woman here to see you. She says she's your new associate..."

"My new ..." I start and then stop when I remember I told Craig to tell Serena to come in today at nine and it's now, I glance at my watch, eight fifty-five. Good. At least she knows how to keep time. "Ok, send her in please."

"Wait, you mean it's true?" Ruth says, her eyes widening.

"Yes," I reply. "Sorry Ruth, I forgot all about it or I would have told you."

"Oh, that's ok," she says with a slight frown. "What about HR and stuff?"

"Yeah, I know. She's the daughter of a friend. You sort everything out with her later, won't you?"

"Right. Of course. I'll send her in now."

I nod and turn to my computer. Knowing I won't have time to do everything I wanted to do now, I decide that the phone calls can wait. I will catch a cab to my first offsite meeting later on today rather than driving and get caught up on my way there and for now, I'll start on my most important emails.

I open the most important one and start typing my response. I'm almost done when there's another knock on my office door.

"Come in," I call. When the door opens, I don't look up. "Take a seat Serena, I will be with you in two minutes. I just need to send this email."

"Ok," she says.

I sense her moving towards my desk and sitting down opposite me as I finish up the email. Her scent wafts towards me – vanilla and something else I can't place, maybe orange?

Whatever it is, it smells good, and I find myself taking longer, deeper breaths to breathe it in. I finish the email and hit send with a bit of a flourish and then I look up and smile at Serena. She smiles back and for a second, I feel like everything stops.

This beautiful woman in front of me is not the Serena I remember. Where the old Serena was plump, this Serena is voluptuous, with curves in all the right places. Her breasts are big but pert and I can't wait for her to stand up so I can check out her ass. Where the old Serena wore glasses that dwarfed her face, the new Serena wears sexy, black framed rectangular shaped glasses that fit her face properly and draw attention to her huge, bright green eyes. Her hair is still curly, but it's a few shades darker and the frizz that used to sort of float all around her head has been tamed and her hair frames her face nicely.

In short, I might as well just say it. Serena got hot. Like really fucking hot. She has left behind that awkward teenage phase and turned into a beautiful young woman. It's a good job I don't mix business and pleasure and it's a really good job I don't go around fucking anyone that's related to my best friend, because if I didn't have those rules in place, I think I could be in real trouble with this one.

I realize I'm staring at her, and I force myself to smile and act like everything is normal.

"How are you, Serena? It's been a while since I've seen you," I say.

"I'm good thank you," she replies. "It's been ages, hasn't it? I guess between my studies and your work it makes sense we'd keep missing each other. How are you?"

"Good," I say with a smile. "Now I don't mean to sound rude, but I'm kind of pushed for time so we'll have to get straight into it."

"Of course," Serena agrees with a smile. "And for the record, I don't think that's rude."

"So, you graduated from Harvard, right?" I ask.

Serena nods.

"Yes," she says. "With a degree in business management and marketing."

"And did that involve any sort of on-the-job training?" I ask.

"Yes, but ..." Serena says but then she shakes her head. "Nothing."

"Come on," I say. "Spill it."

It's obvious by her facial expression that she wants to say more but she's not sure how I'm going to take it.

"I don't want to sound pretentious," she says. "But I found the places Harvard sent us to for our placements weren't that great. Like, don't get me wrong, they were huge advertising agencies, and they would be good places to work, but as far as training went, they were too busy to really show us anything and all we really did was sit around watching them or doing shit jobs like filing and making endless cups of coffee."

She pushes an orange-colored file folder across the desk and smiles shyly.

"I took it upon myself to do some intern work at smaller firms through the holidays and I found those much more useful. I was even given some small projects of my own to work on," she says.

I pick up the folder and flick through the sheets inside of it. It's good. Better than I expected if I'm honest. I know Craig said he'd seen Serena's stuff and it was good, but he's biased and I'm not. But in this case, we agree.

"This is really good," I say.

Serena blushes slightly and smiles and I can't help but notice how cute she is when her cheeks flush pink. I wonder if her cheeks would be that color post orgasm. I push that thought firmly away and focus on the file. I come across a story board for a TV ad for a soft drinks company and I frown as I try to place why it is familiar and then it hits me. It's an actual TV ad that gets shown now and again currently.

"Did you come up with all of this?" I ask Serena, nodding down at the story board.

"Not the branding or the logo," she says. "But I came up with the story and the script for the actual commercial. I have done branding for other companies though."

I nod. I see that. I flick through the rest of the sheets in the folder, but it's just out of curiosity really at this point. I have already seen enough to know that Serena is a good hire. The only thing is, the only opening I have right now is for someone to be my associate and I'm too busy to do much with her today. I don't want her to think my firm is like one of those faceless firms that Harvard sent her to though where interns are largely ignored and don't learn anything.

I think for a minute, and I decide to take a measured risk. I lean down and open my third drawer down on my desk and pull out a thin file which I place on the desk. I close my drawer and smile at Serena.

"I think I've seen enough to know that you won't need hand holding a lot. Don't worry, I still plan on mentoring you and helping you to develop your skills. But today I am in back-to-back meetings and I'm not sure the next few days are any better. So, I'm going to give you the sort of chance most associates would only be able to dream of, but I think you can handle it," I say.

"Ok," Serena says when I pause to gauge her reaction.

She's leaning forward, engaged, and interested in what I'm saying. I like that and so I carry on.

"I'm going to give you Hislop's stuff to work on. They are a brand-new start up and right now, they are selling a very niche kind of dog food. In time, they hope to branch out to other dog foods and then maybe to foods for other animals, but they aren't trying to run before they can walk, so right now, we're focusing on this one thing. They need a brand – logo, ethos, billboard campaigns, social media campaigns and a TV ad. Do you think you can handle all of that?" I ask.

Serena's face breaks into a wide smile and I notice how much it lights up her eyes, how the green sparkles and how pretty she looks. I tell myself not to think like that, but how can I not? It's like saying there's a red box; don't notice that it's red though.

"Yes," she says. "I really do."

"Good," I say.

I push the folder towards her, and she picks it up and scans over the information sheets inside. She smiles again, her excitement at having her own project clear to see on her face. She looks back up from the folder and smiles at me.

"I can definitely do this," she says. "I promise I won't let you down."

I nod and return her smile.

"I'm sure you won't," I say. I glance at my watch and then I look back at Serena. "I really wanted to be able to spend more time with you on your first day, but I have to head out really soon. I will have Ruth show you around. You've met Ruth, right? My personal assistant?"

Serena nods.

"Good," I say. "For today, if you have any questions or if you need anything, just ask Ruth. Obviously, her speciality isn't marketing, but we have worked together a long time and I trust her opinion on most things, and I think she knows me well enough to know if I would approve something or not."

"Ok, that sounds great," Serena says with a smile.

"Do you have any questions?" I ask.

She shakes her head.

"No," she says. "Not right now."

For the first time since she came into my office, she looks down at her hands in her lap as she speaks instead of looking at me.

"Serena," I say gently. I wait for her to look back up at me before I carry on. "Please don't be worried about asking questions or speaking up. I like people who know their own mind and who aren't afraid to speak up ok?"

She nods.

"Ok, then yes, I have a question. Well, actually, it's more of a favor to ask of you," she says.

It's far too early in her time here for her to be asking for favors and I'm reminded once more that Serena is a family member of my best friend. Is she going to expect preferential treatment? Because if she is, she's going to be massively disappointed. Despite that, I am curious as to what she thinks it's acceptable to ask for already and so I nod for her to go on.

"I was hoping we could keep it between us that we already know each other. I know I'm probably just being paranoid, but I don't want anyone thinking I'm only here because of that. I mean I get that at the moment, that is the only reason, but I want to prove myself with my work," she says.

Ok, I admit I misjudged her. That's the sort of favor I can get behind. In fact, I am relieved she feels that way because I don't want to have to spend any time second guessing myself if people think I'm being too lenient on her, because if no one knows that we know each other, and I am too lenient, I have no doubt someone will let me know. It also means that if Serena is working with someone else, they won't give her an easy ride thinking that's what I would want.

"Yes, that's perfectly fine," I say with a smile. "Let's just keep work and our personal lives separate."

Serena smiles gratefully and nods.

"Thank you," she says.

"No problem. Right, if that's it for questions, I'll get Ruth back in here," I say.

Serena nods again, confirming that's it for questions and I call through to Ruth and ask her to come back to my office. In less than a minute, there's a knock on my office door and I call out for the person knocking to come in. The door opens and Ruth steps inside, closing the door quietly behind her. She walks towards my desk and seeing there's no chair for her, she perches on the edge of my desk. I would have preferred her to get another chair, but I let it go. I don't want to undermine her in front of Serena on Serena's first day here.

"So, obviously you two have already met," I say. "But just to make it official, Ruth, this is Serena West, my new associate. Serena, this is Ruth Stainsby, my personal assistant."

The women smile at each other. They both look a little uncertain, but I guess that's normal until they get to know each other a little bit.

"Ruth, I've just been explaining to Serena that I am up to my eyes with meetings and what not for the next few days and I have said that she should come to you with any questions or anything she might have," I say. "And if you could just check in on her now and again, make sure she's on the right track, that sort of thing, that would be a big help."

"Yes, of course," Ruth replies.

"Serena is going to be working on the Hislop's campaign," I tell Ruth.

"Alone?" Ruth asks, raising an eyebrow.

"She's more than qualified to do the work, don't worry," I say. "But she won't be on her own will she, because you'll be there to help her if she needs it."

Ruth smiles and nods, but again, her smile looks strained.

I sigh. I don't have time for this, but I need to know if there is some sort of problem.

"What's wrong?" I ask Ruth.

"Nothing," she says.

"Then what's with the face?" I ask her.

She looks away from me for a moment and then she looks down at the desk.

"I'm just not sure I should be the one looking after Serena. I've never done anything marketing related. Should she not be with one of the marketing executives?" Ruth says.

Well, I wasn't expecting that. This morning is definitely full of surprises. What I mistook for hostility on Ruth's part was actually self-doubt. I have never known Ruth to doubt herself so I can be forgiven for not recognizing it I suppose.

"Serena is more than able to hit the ground running on the marketing side," I say. "Anything she needs to ask you is going to be more system based, or maybe where to find something. But if you do take a look at the campaign now and again, you know my tastes and you know the brand's values. I trust you to know if I would be happy with the campaign at hand or not."

Ruth's smile widens and she looks up at me once more.

"Then consider it done," she says. She turns to Serena with the same happy smile on her face. "Are you ready for a tour of the building then?"

CHAPTER 3
Serena

I smile politely at Ruth as she offers me a tour of the building. She doesn't like me, and I don't know why. She covered it well when Wyatt noticed something was off, but not well enough to fool me. I don't know what to make of her. I don't know if she's not a very nice person, or if the whole ice queen thing she's been doing is just like her work persona or what. I know I will have to hit the ground running here and be willing to work things out for myself though, because I really don't want to have to ask this woman for her help.

On the other hand, it's a shame Wyatt is going to be busy over the next few days because holy shit, would I be happy to have to ask for his help. My mind can't help but wander and I see myself walking into Wyatt's office, naked except for my bra and panties.

"Can you help me?" I ask in a husky voice that isn't my real voice, but I wish it was. "You see, I am almost at orgasm, but something is stopping me from getting there."

Wyatt stands up from his desk chair and comes around to the front of his desk and he beckons me to him. I eagerly oblige and he wraps his arms around me and pulls me close and kisses me. As he kisses me, he pushes my panties to one side and works my clit until I come, screaming his name, and soaking his hand and the cuff of his shirt sleeve. Oops.

I have always had a crush on Wyatt for as long as I can remember. He was my cool Uncle Craig's even cooler friend, and he was handsome in a way that boys my age just weren't. But this is different now. This isn't like a crush; this is a serious attraction. I don't know how any straight woman could look at the perfection that is Wyatt and not have a serious attraction to him.

He's tall and broad shouldered and even when he's fully dressed, I can see his defined muscles pushing against his clothes, like even his body knows it is perfection and wants to be shown off. He has light grey eyes, and they stand out against his tanned skin and dark hair. He has a square jaw and cheekbones to die for, and the smattering of stubble he is sporting is so fucking hot I feel wet just looking at him. It's so hard to look at him and not imagine straddling him, riding his cock.

But I know I can't act on these urges. Wyatt has never shown the slightest bit of interest in me sexually and I am not going to be that girl that throws herself at her uncle's friend and gets rejected. Talk about tragic. Especially now that I'm working for him. No, I will have to stick to craving for Wyatt from afar – that part hasn't changed since before I went away to college. I don't know how long I can be around Wyatt without acting on the lust I feel when I look at him though.

"Serena? Are you coming?" Ruth says.

Give me two minutes alone with Wyatt and I would be, I think to myself. Of course, I don't say that and when I feel my cheeks turn pink from my dirty thoughts, I'm sure that my blush will be mistaken for embarrassment that I was off in a world of my own while Ruth was talking to me.

"Yes, sorry," I say. I get to my feet and smile quickly at Wyatt. "Thank you."

He nods at me, and I follow Ruth out of his office. As the door shuts behind me, I feel an overwhelming urge to open it again and slip back inside there with him. It certainly seems like a better prospect than following Ruth around, but I remind myself of how hard I have worked to get my degree and my portfolio, and I won't throw this opportunity away.

I follow Ruth to the elevator, and we wait for it. When it comes, we get inside and go to the ground floor. The elevator takes us there and pings and the doors open. Ruth steps out of the elevator car and I follow her.

"Did you drive here?" she asks.

"Yeah," I say.

"And I take it you found the staff parking lot? Just if you are parking in the wrong one, you will have to pay," she says.

"I found it thank you," I say and smile at her. She smiles back but it doesn't meet her eyes.

"Well," she says, gesturing in a circle around herself with her arms to encompass the space we are standing in. "This is the lobby and the main reception desk. That's the waiting area for clients or potential clients if they come for meetings or presentations or whatever. That's pretty much it for this floor. There's a staff bathroom and a small kitchen but you won't be working on this floor, so I doubt you'll ever need those."

She's leading me back to the elevator as she talks and I can't help but notice how good she looks in her dress, how her legs go on for days. She looks like she's just stepped out of the pages of Vogue. And then there's me in my safe, sensible pants suit. I know for tomorrow that I can dress a bit nicer though and I plan to.

We go to the first floor and Ruth points to her left.

"That's our IT department," she says. She points to the right. "Down there, you've got all of our conference rooms." I make a mental note of those as that definitely sounds like something I might need. "All of them are labelled so don't worry about trying to remember which one is which at this point." I nod my understanding, grateful that it sounds like the building is going to be easy enough to navigate. "There are breakroom facilities and what not along there for the staff working on this floor too. And right at the end of that corridor is our HR department. Any questions?"

I shake my head and Ruth leads me back to the elevator once more. We go up one more floor. All three of the main floors are laid out the same, with one decent sized area at the left of the stairs and then a long corridor with plenty of smaller rooms off the right-hand side. Only the lobby is different for obvious reasons.

"That's the finance department," Ruth says. "They sort wages, taxes, that kind of thing. Once you get set up in your office today, pop on down here and tell them you're new. They'll email you some forms to fill in and get you in the system and then each week, first thing on a Monday morning, you need to send them your timecard for the last week with your hours worked on it. If you fail to send the card in and you are not on authorized leave, it will be assumed you weren't at work and you won't be paid. Got it?"

"Got it," I reply, making a mental note to never forget to submit my timecard.

"On that side of this floor is the main marketing department. You'll find associates and executives down there," Ruth says.

She doesn't make it sound particularly important, but I think for me, it could be a life saver. Beyond that door are

18

people doing what I'm doing only with more experience. If I ever need to pick anyone's brains or get an opinion on a tagline or something, those are my people. And surely at least some of them are bound to be nicer than Ruth, therefore more approachable if I do need any help on my campaign.

My campaign. I feel a tingling in my stomach when I think about that. I still can't believe it's my first day here and I already have my own campaign to work on.

Ruth leads me back to the elevator and we go back to the third floor where Wyatt's office, and presumably mine and Ruth's offices are. Ruth points to the little end first.

"The bathroom, kitchen and breakroom are all along there," she says. "You'll find the selection of snacks and drinks to be of a much higher standard on this floor than the others. There is a huge fridge in the kitchen, and it is kept pretty much fully stocked with snacks and sodas. There is a hot drinks machine that does loads of different coffees, tea, hot chocolate, and some other bits. Help yourself to anything you want out of the big fridge. Wyatt provides that for us. If you bring any of your own food in that needs refrigerating, there's a small refrigerator near the sink you can use."

"Ok, thank you," I say.

"The break room opens off the other side of the kitchen. It's comfortable and you will definitely enjoy your breaks there. But don't get too comfortable and forget to come back to work or anything," Ruth says with a laugh that sounds fake to me.

I laugh too, my laughter equally fake. I've done nothing to her, and she's decided to take a dislike to me. Well, two can play that game honey. She must be sure she's been beat because she goes back to the tour.

"Along here," she says, as we start walking along the corridor we left from, "Is the top marketing executive offices.

The deeper in you get, the more senior they are. You'll also find the CFO and the VP along here too. Right at the end is Wyatt's office and mine is next to his."

I nod. I remember that much from this morning.

"And this here is your office," she says.

She pushes the door open and stands back gesturing with her arm for me to enter first. I step inside and I am immediately awed at the size of the office. It's big enough for the whole ground floor of my house to fit inside of it, I'm sure.

The floor is a thick, plush black carpet with tiny flecks of silver that catch the light and make it look like a disco ball is spinning above it. Three black leather chairs and a black leather couch are arranged around a glass and chrome coffee table underneath the window. In the center of the office, is a huge mahogany desk and a black leather computer chair opposite two mahogany chairs with softer looking, black leather covered cushions on the seat part and the back rests. I look around and despite wanting to remain cold with Ruth I can't help but grin at her.

"This is amazing," I say.

"It's one of the nicer offices, one that Wyatt keeps solely for his associates," she says. She flashes me another fake smile. "You know where my office is right? Right next door to Wyatt's. She doesn't give me a chance to reply to her and then she speaks like she's bragging about her proximity to Wyatt.

"Yeah, I know where you are," I say.

"Good," Ruth says. "Then why not get settled in and then start on your project. And don't forget to visit the finances department at some point today to make sure you are in the system in time to be paid for this week."

"I won't forget. Thank you," I say.

Ruth nods to me and then she slips out of the office closing the door behind her and leaving me alone in my office.

CHAPTER 4

Serena

My office. Wow. I take a moment to just smile and take it all in and then I put the file about Hislop's on my desk and I hang my handbag up on the coat hooks beside the door and I slip my jacket off and hang it up next to my handbag.

I just stand there for a moment, still needing that extra bit of time for taking it all in and then I debate going down to the finance department to get the forms Ruth said I would need. I check my watch and decide to make a start on a vision board for the brand first and then I will grab the forms just before lunch and I can fill them out as I eat.

My decision made; I sit down at my desk. I move my chair up and then down slightly until it's the right height for me and then I reach out to switch my computer on. I hit the start-up button, but nothing happens. I frown and try again. Nothing. I lift the receiver of my desk phone and hear the dial tone so there isn't any sort of power outage. I think for a moment and then with a sigh, I get onto my hands and knees and crawl underneath the desk. I guess the pants suit isn't the worst idea then, because doing this in a skirt or dress would be so much worse.

I look at the tangle of wires and sigh. It's going to take a while to work out what should be where and if anything is missing, but it's not like I have any other choice and so I pick a wire at random and follow it, untangling it as I go. The wire I choose seems to be connected properly at both ends and so I move on to the next one. I am onto wire number four when I find the problem. The end has slipped out of the base unit. I look at the back of it and match the shape of the wire with the shape of the outlet on the base unit and I push it in.

I crawl back out of the gap, and still on my knees, I try the power button again. This time, it works and the computer fires into life. I smile, pleased with myself for solving this. I crawl back underneath the desk and screw the cable into place. I wonder how it came loose. It's not like it could have been accidentally caught with someone's toe and been pulled out without that person noticing. You have to unscrew it to get it loose. I wonder if Wyatt's last associate left in a huff.

I don't really care if they did. It means nothing to me. Just because they couldn't hack the job doesn't mean I won't be able to. And if I can't, I already know I won't be doing anything as petty as unplugging part of the computer.

I get back up onto my feet and dust off the knees of my pants and then I sit down in front of my desk again. The power up continues and then the Windows screen appears asking me for a login. Fuck. I don't have a login.

I debate searching through the drawers and everything for a login, but even if I found one jotted down somewhere, it wouldn't be mine, it would be my predecessor's and that's no use to me. I need my own. I debate going to Ruth, but what's the point of that? She'll only tell me to contact the IT department surely. So that's what I'll do. And if I do already have a login set up and Ruth has just forgotten to give me the details, then I'm sure IT will know that and be able to give me those details.

I leave my office, leaving behind my handbag and jacket, taking only a small notepad and a pen to write my login down on. I go down to the first floor and go and tap on the door of the IT department. No one answers my knock and I realize I'm being a bit silly. The IT department is unlikely to have a secretary for the main door – it's not like they will have clients visiting them – and so I open the door and step inside of the department.

The room is less busy than I expected. I can see a huge glass walled room full of servers with flashing blue and green lights. There are several offices after the server room and then the rest of the area is open plan with the employees sitting in their own little cubicles at a centralized desk. There are only three people currently sitting at the desk and one of them is on a phone call. Another one looks up at the sound of the door closing behind me. He smiles at me, and I smile back.

"Hi," I say. "I'm sorry, I don't know what the procedure is, but I'm new here and I don't have any login details for my computer."

"Well let's get that fixed for you," he says. "Come on over here. I'm Adam by the way."

I move closer and sit down on the seat from the cubicle next to Adam's.

"What's your name and position and your location within the building?" Adam says.

"I'm Serena West and I am Wyatt's new associate. I work on the third floor," I say.

"Oh, you are office royalty," Adam laughs.

I laugh with him, not wanting him to think I'm taking myself too seriously. He turns away from me and types away on his keyboard, clicking about and typing and then clicking some more until he finally stops and looks back at me and smiles.

"All sorted," he says.

"Thank you," I say. I go to ask him for the details but luckily, he speaks first, and I manage to avoid embarrassing myself with my question.

"So, I've obviously done you a main login so you can get onto the server. I've set you up an email account and I've given you logins for all the programs I think you will need," Adam says. "I've sent a document with all those logins to your printer. The first time you use each one, it will prompt you to change the password. Do this and don't disclose the password to anyone else. And if you find you have any other programs you need access to, my extension number is on the printout so you can call me or pop back in and I'll get you sorted."

"Thank you, Adam," I say. "You have no idea how helpful you've been."

"Anytime," he says.

I smile again and then I get up and leave the room. I decide to head to the finance department while I am out of the office anyway and so I walk up a floor rather than using the elevator. I find the finance department and go in and introduce myself to the first person I see who turns out to be a payroll clerk and can add me to the payment system and send me everything I need to fill in.

"What's your email address?" the payroll clerk asks.

"I don't know," I say, cringing as I admit to this. "I've literally just come from the IT department where Adam has just sorted all my logins and an email address for me. He's sent them to my printer, but I haven't been back to my office yet."

"Not to worry, I'm sure I can crack it. Unless your name is super common," she says.

"I don't think it's that common," I say. "It's Serena West."

She types and then looks up at me and smiles.

"You're right. You're the only Serena and the only West on our directory. So, your email address is going to be Serena dot West at Smart Marketing Solutions dot com. I've sent you a bunch of forms there. If you haven't received them, or for some reason your email address is something different, pop back down and we'll sort it," she says.

"Thank you," I say.

I check my watch as I climb the final flight of stairs back up to my floor. It's not even twelve o'clock yet and I have managed to get myself online and sort my paperwork for the finance team. Not a bad start Serena, I tell myself.

CHAPTER 5

Serena

I go back to my office and go straight to my printer where sure enough, a printout of logins is sitting there waiting for me. I enter the details into the main sign on screen and I am rewarded with the sight of a desktop. It has a fair few folders and files and I have no idea if they might turn out to be important or not, so I make a new folder and title it *Not my circus* and then I put all the files and folders in it so that I am starting anew.

I remember what Adam said and I change my main login's password and jot the new one down on the printout and then I go to the company email and find that the payroll clerk was spot on about my email address. I find her email and quickly download all the forms I need to complete.

I get them all done and sent back and then I change the password on my email account and note that down too. I login to the main software next, a nice, all in one design solution where I can design graphics and mood boards and branding boards and ads and everything I ever dreamed of, all in one place. I quickly change my password and note down the new one and then I put the cheat sheet in my top drawer. At least those are empty. I was half expecting to find the person before me to have left things in the drawers after seeing the mess left behind on the desktop of the computer.

I pick up the Hislop's file and read through the notes. There isn't a whole lot of detail because the brand is trusting us to appeal to their target market for them. I like that because it means I can do my thing and help them properly. I hate it when I am asked to do a campaign, but the client has put all these caveats in and ultimately, they get in the way of my work. I have never understood the logic of someone who pays an expert to do something for them but then ties their hands and won't let them do it the right way.

What I gather from the short brief is that Hislop's is brand new and that is it a high end, more expensive brand than what is currently available. They are hoping to appeal to the owners of show dogs, stud dogs and those owners with plenty of spare cash and lots of love for their fur babies who only want the best of everything.

I start by doing a mood board and then as things begin to clarify for me, I write a company mission statement that I think fits the brand perfectly. I start working on colors and font choices next and once I am happy with those, I design the logo and the packaging for the food.

My stomach is rumbling by the time I have finished, and I check the time. I am shocked to see it is almost three pm. The day has flown by so far, but I'm not surprised I am hungry. I get up and grab my handbag and go to the kitchen. I feel weird going into the fridge and helping myself but that's what Ruth said it was for and so I open it and peer in.

I take a can of soda and a cheese and ham baguette, and I go and sit down at one of the tables. I eat the sandwich and drink the soda and then I go to the lady's room. I use the toilet and then I wash my hands and study my reflection. I like who

I see looking back at me. She looks confident and happy, her cheeks slightly pink and her mouth locked in a permanent smile.

I spread a bit of pink lip gloss over my lips and run my fingers through my curls, teasing them back into place and then I head back to my office. I've barely sat back down when there is a knock on my office door. My first visitor. I smile to myself and then I shout come in and the door opens. Ruth comes in and I smile at her. She smiles back and I think that maybe I was wrong about her earlier. That smile seemed to meet her eyes.

"How are things going? Are you finding your feet alright?" Ruth asks me as she plonks herself down in one of the chairs opposite mine. "I'm sorry I didn't get to come and check in on you earlier, but I've been busy."

"Oh, that's ok, I've been busy myself," I say. "First of all, there was a loose cable on my computer, then I got that fixed and the computer on and I had no logins, so I went down to IT and got that taken care of. I also went to finance while I was out and about and got all that side of things set up. And then I've been working on the branding for Hislop's."

Ruth raises an eyebrow and then smiles her ice queen smile at me. Great, we're back to this again, I think but don't say.

"You definitely have been busy," she says. "It sounds like you don't need me. Most new starters panic if they don't have a login and come running for someone."

I swear when I mentioned the cable and then the login, Ruth's expression changed. I told myself I was imagining it, but that, coupled with her words now make me think I wasn't imagining it at all. I think Ruth pulled that cable out and I think she was supposed to get my login details sorted but didn't, because she wanted me to panic and look stupid and not get enough done. Well, if that was her game, it backfired and hopefully showed her that she's wasting her time playing silly games with me.

"Oh, I find that hard to believe," I say with a smile. "It is really just common sense isn't it – you need something computer related; you ask the IT department."

"I think some new starters are worried about overstepping their roles," Ruth says.

"I get that," I say. "But I figured if I needed my request authorized by someone higher up, the IT department would have told me that and I didn't want to disturb anyone unnecessarily. Anyway, it's all sorted now so let's not worry about it."

Ruth looks taken aback that I have basically just dismissed any further questions or comments she might have had.

"Of course," she says, smiling tightly. "So, you're up and running and you've completed your forms for finance. I take it you'll be starting to look at your client's brief soon?"

"I've already made a good start on that actually," I say.

"Well, you clearly don't need my help then," Ruth says. "I may as well just leave you to it."

I should just let her go, but I can't do it. As much as she's a bitch and I don't owe her a thing, I still somehow end up feeling bad for her and I shake my head.

"No," I say. "Of course, I still need your help. In fact, I'd be grateful if you would take a quick look at what I've done so far while you're here."

"Ok," Ruth says.

She waits while I open the first file. I turn my screen so that we can both see it and I talk her through my thinking with the brand aesthetics and their mission statement. Ruth nods along with me and when I've finished, she smiles at me.

"That's really good, Serena," she says. "You definitely

understand the brand and who their target consumer is and how to appeal to them. Wyatt will be very pleased with this. Of course, he might make the odd tweak here and there as is his right, but overall, I'm confident that he will approve this."

"Thank you," I say, relieved to hear that, especially from Ruth. It must be true if Ruth is saying it. There's no way she'd give me praise if she didn't have to and I don't think she'd let me send something awful to Wyatt, because she would as much to blame as I would be if she had signed off on it.

"Well, I'll leave you to it then, you know where I am if you do need anything else," Ruth says. I thank her again and she moves towards the door to my office. She starts to open it and then she turns back to me. "Oh. I almost forgot. Like I said everything you have there is good, but when you come to write the pitch, don't forget to mention the advantages of vegetarianism in dogs."

"Vegetarianism?" I asked.

She rolls her eyes good naturedly and laughs.

"I know. It's crazy right. They're dogs. Give them meat and have done with it. But this company's unique selling point, USP for short, is vegetarian food for dogs so make sure you make a big point about this and the benefits of it," she says.

"Ok, I will," I say.

CHAPTER 6

Serena

I'm shocked that I missed such a big detail, and I'm also a tad disappointed because my lovely little campaign just got one whole hell of a lot harder, and I can see why Wyatt palmed it off on me now. This brand needs more than an ad expert. The USP might appeal to vegans and the odd tree hugger, but generally speaking, people aren't going to spend extra money on dog food for it to not even be meat.

I read back through the file again once Ruth has gone and there is nothing in there to even suggest that the food is vegetarian. I shake my head. Is that another of Ruth's sabotages of me? Was she supposed to have told me this from the beginning but decided to slow me down? If that was her plan, she has failed miserably because she's still told me before I write the pitch and all I really need to do is add a small box with the words one hundred percent meat free in it on the packaging. It will only take me a few seconds to correct it.

I open my designs and add the bubble about the food being one hundred percent meat free and then I go off to the internet to do some research. I need to find out which experts are now recommending a vegetarian diet for dogs, and I need to find out who is endorsing it. I struggle to find anything. I do find a few articles that explain that giving dogs vegetables and some fruits can make their coats shinier and help their general health, it still doesn't say anything about replacing their meat with vegetables though. It just talks about adding the vegetables in alongside the meat. Great. Just great. We're not even going to be able to appeal to those people who will do anything if they think an expert has recommended it.

There's really not much I can do with this except to do what I can with the information I have and by the end of the day, I know mostly where I am going with the campaign and how I am going to incorporate the vegetarian stuff.

The day has flown by, and I am shocked when I see that it's already past going home time. I don't mind working late when it's necessary, but I genuinely think I've done a good day's work today and besides, I'm meeting Brook, my best friend, for dinner tonight. My plan was to go home and shower and change before meeting Brook, but I don't have enough time for that now. If I hurry up, I have enough time to get to the restaurant on time.

I shut my computer down and collect my handbag and jacket from the coat hooks and then I leave my office, closing the door behind me. I hurry to the elevators and go down in them. I'm halfway across the lobby when it hits me that I am perhaps meant to ask Ruth's permission to leave, or at least let her know that I'm going. I don't have time to go back and tell her now, so I'll find out for tomorrow. It's not like I've snuck out early so I don't feel guilty or anything.

I leave the building and go and get into my car and drive across town to the restaurant I'm meeting Brook at. I manage to step inside with just one minute to spare before I'm classified as late.

Brook spots me straight away as I make my way towards the dining area of the restaurant, and she stands up and waves to me and I make my way over to the table and we both sit down. I put my purse down on the carpet between my feet and then I fight my way out of my jacket and hang it over the back of my chair. Brook smiles at me.

"You look flustered," she says.

"I am flustered," I say, talking too quickly because my nerves are all over the place. I take a deep breath and I go on. I am still talking too fast, but I feel a bit calmer now that I'm here and sitting down. "I was all organized and I knew what time I needed to leave the office to be on time to meet you and then the day just ran away with me."

"Well, you're not technically late yet so I forgive you," Brook says with a smile which I return. "And I guess on your first day you can't bolt out as soon as the clock strikes five, right? You did ok girl. You showed that you were willing to work over when it was needed, and you still managed to be on time to meet me. Give yourself a break, ok?

"Right. Ok. I will. Thank you for understanding," I say, meaning it. It's good that she's not making a big deal out of this. In fact, if anything, she seems to think I am overreacting because I'm not properly late yet anyway.

Brook waves away my thank you with a flick of one wrist and a muttered "behave" and then she grins at me excitedly.

"Well? How did your first day go? Tell me everything," Brook says. Her smile widens. "Tell me all about Hot Wyatt. Is he still hot?"

"Oh Brook, he's every bit as gorgeous as I remember him to be only like a thousand times hotter if that is even possible. I am in serious trouble with him," I say dreamily.

"Yeah, but you're not a kid anymore," Brook says. "You can actually act on it now."

"Not a chance," I say, shaking my head in horror at the very thought of it.

"Why not?" Brook asks.

She looks genuinely surprised to hear that I won't be pursuing Wyatt, but I get why she's surprised. If I looked like her, I probably would pursue him. Brook is tall, thin, and blonde. She has pretty blue eyes and a cute little nose and just right lips. In short, she is hot, and she would never have to worry about being rejected by a guy she liked because it just wouldn't happen.

"Because the only thing I can think of that's worse than embarrassing myself in front of a family friend, is embarrassing myself in front of a family friend who I also work for," I say, going back to her question. "God, imagine how bad it would be if I like threw myself at him and then I had to see him every day after he had turned me down."

We stop talking for a moment as a waiter approaches our table. He is wearing black trousers and a crisp white shirt with a long black tie. His dark hair is short and spiky, and he doesn't look very old, perhaps in his late teens or very early twenties. He's cute in that shy sort of way that I would have liked when I was young enough to have dated him.

"The usual?" Brook asks me and I nod. She smiles up at the waiter. "Can we please have two gin and tonics, one with lemon and one with lime, both with ice please. And then a portion of the potato skins with sour cream and a portion of garlic mushrooms for starters, followed by lasagna and chips and fish and chips for mains and finally, two sticky toffee puddings for dessert please, one with ice cream, one with custard."

"Wow," the waiter smiles after he finishes scribbling down everything Brook said. "I wish everyone was this organized. You don't even have a menu."

"What can I say. We're regulars," Brook says with a grin and a shrug.

The waiter laughs and starts away from the table.

"Your drinks will be along in a second and your food won't be too long after that," he says.

Brook turns her attention back to me when the waiter is gone and carries on the conversation like there hasn't been a pause.

"I wasn't suggesting you throw yourself at him," Brook says, rolling her eyes. "Honestly Serena. Since when have I ever suggested you should go around throwing yourself at people. I like to think we have a little bit more class than that. I was simply suggesting you subtly let him know that you are open to dating him and then let him do the leg work."

"Oh Brook, you know I'm not good at that kind of stuff," I say, shaking my head. "I'm awful at subtle. I would literally end up throwing myself at him and not even realize I hadn't been subtle until he laughed at me."

"He wouldn't laugh at you. But that's not the point. The point is that you could be good at it though. You don't actually know you're not good at it because you won't try it," she says. "How many times have I shown you how to do it?"

"Yeah, but you're you. This Goddess. And I'm me. Just little pudgy Serena. Of course, it works for you," I say. "You could just stand there and say and do nothing and guys would try it on with you."

"Ok," Brook says, ticking her points off on her fingers as she goes. "Yes, I'm me. I'm not a Goddess but thank you anyway. Yes, you're you. You are not pudgy. You are gorgeous and you have lovely big boobs and hips that guys want to touch. It works for me because I am confident. We just need to work on your confidence."

I sigh and shake my head. It's not my confidence that's the

problem. I'm not so much not confident as I am a realist. I'm not one of those girls who thinks they are hideous - I just think Wyatt is out of my league and he is.

CHAPTER 7

Serena

The waiter comes back with our drinks, and our starters, I think that is a good thing because it'll give me a break from Brook trying to get me to be sexy when I'm not. I'm not wrong.

"Hey," Brook says to the waiter. She picks up a mushroom and bites it in a rather suggestive manner. Then she nods at me. "If you were sitting opposite her and she did that to you and maybe ran her toe up your leg beneath the table and then said 'oops'. Would it turn you on?"

"Brook," I hiss, feeling my face burning up.

"Oh, don't be embarrassed," she says. She turns back to the waiter. "Just hypothetically. She's not trying to get you to go out with her or anything. She has her sights set on this guy and she doesn't know how to show him she's interested. Serena, do what I just did with one of those potato skins."

"No way," I say and shake my head.

"Oh, go on. Don't be a bore," Brook says.

I hate it when she says I'm a bore. It usually means I won't go along with another of her bright ideas, but it still hurts. I sigh and pick up a potato skin. I look at it in a way I hope is sexy and then I look in the waiter's eyes and nibble on the potato skin. Instant regret seizes me as it burns my tongue and I make an ahh sound and grab my drink.

"It's ok. You don't have to answer," Brook says with a sigh and the waiter practically runs from us.

"So maybe when you try this on Wyatt, you use cold food," Brook says.

"Or maybe I just wait and see if he shows any interest in me," I say. "And not traumatize him like I have that poor waiter."

"See, with some guys that could work, but not with Wyatt," Brook says.

She announces it like it's a fact and I have to know how she's so sure.

"Why is that?" I ask.

"Because he's friends with your dad Serena. He is not going to expect a young, gorgeous woman such as yourself to want to date him unless you make it clear," she says. "Just your age alone makes you way out of his league and he knows it."

"Wait. Are you seriously saying that Wyatt will think I am the one out of his league? Honestly Brook, you haven't seen this guy," I say.

"I've seen a hundred Wyatt's," Brook says. "Show him that you are interested, and he will be so grateful for the attention that he will be putty in your hands."

"I'll try," I lie.

I nibble on a potato skin and think for a moment. I don't want to lie to Brook but she won't let this go until she thinks I am going to let Wyatt know I like him, and I have no intention of doing that because like I said to her earlier, it's too embarrassing.

"Yes," Brook says, clapping her hands together and making me jump. She grins and nods. "You've got it."

"Got what?" I ask.

"The sexy nibble," she says.

"Oh. I was just a million miles away," I say with a laugh.

"Well do that when you next see Wyatt. And you can't possibly say that will be embarrassing if he doesn't take the hint. Just tell him the same thing as you just told me – you were a million miles away and not paying attention to what you were doing," she says.

That's not her worst idea, but I still think it would make working together pretty damned awkward afterwards if he told me he wasn't interested and I asked why he randomly said that and he says I was eating my lunch in a sexy way and I say nope, I was just a million miles away. God it would almost be worse than me just saying I like him and him rejecting me.

"Right. Enough about me. Tell me about your date last night," I say.

Brook doesn't hold back. She tells me every little detail, even down to how she had to fake an orgasm in the end because he wasn't doing it for her, and she was getting sore.

"He's cute though, so I'll probably see him again, and just hope he's open to a little bit of direction if you get my drift," she says with a twinkle in her eye.

I laugh and nod. God help the poor guy is all I can think to that.

"That's actually a really good argument for dating someone older," Brook says thoughtfully. She flashes me a smile. "They've been about a bit, learned what a woman wants. Maybe I should try it."

"Maybe you should," I say with a laugh.

Brook shakes her head, and a visible shudder goes through her.

"Ugh no thanks. No offense Serena, you do you and all that, but the thought of grey pubes and wrinkly asses puts me right off. I'd rather take someone young and teach them myself," she says. "Doesn't the thought of an old man body put you off?"

"No," I say laughing. "Well, I mean yeah, the one you describe sounds pretty gross. But Wyatt isn't like that. Even with his clothes on you can see he works out. And I mean he's only the same age as my Uncle Craig, so forty-two. It's not like he's a pensioner."

"Ok, so he might not have grey pubes just yet and all of his teeth might still be his own," Brook says with another laugh, and I can't help but laugh with her.

While we are laughing, our waiter brings our main courses and we both thank him. He nods an acknowledgment of our thanks and hurries away. The place isn't that busy and I think he's probably a bit scared of what Brook might ask him to do next after last time he came to the table.

"So, what's the job like? And the people? Other than Hot Grandpa of course," Brook says when the waiter has gone.

I wrinkle my nose up at her.

"Eww. Less of the Hot Grandpa shit," I say with a laugh.

"Just calling it how I see it," Brook giggles. I shake my head and she stops laughing. "Ok, I'll behave. How is the job and the people there other than Hot Wyatt?"

"I love the job," I say. "I really thought I'd be taking a back seat and kind of watching Wyatt work, maybe doing bits and pieces of research for him. But he looked through my portfolio and he said I was already ready for my own campaign. I've been working on it today actually. It's a dog food brand."

"That's amazing," Brook says. "Obviously you're going to smash it. It's good to know you're working somewhere that appreciates you though and not just have you making coffee and shit because you're young."

I nod and pick my glass up and raise it in the air.

"I'll drink to that," I say.

"To smashing it and being appreciated by Hot Wyatt," Brook says with a smirk.

I roll my eyes, but I repeat the cheer anyway. We clink glasses and each take a drink of our drinks and return our glasses to the table.

"So, it sounds like a pretty chill place to work then," Brook says. "What are the others like?"

"I get the impression it's chill yeah, as long as you're doing what you're meant to be doing. Wyatt doesn't seem like the sort of boss who wants to micromanage your every move which is good. I haven't met that many people yet. I've met someone from pay roll who was nice and Adam from IT who was nice and super helpful. And Wyatt's PA, Ruth."

"What's wrong with her?" Brook asks.

"Why should anything be wrong with her?" I ask.

"I don't know," Brook says. "Just the way you said her name. Your voice changed."

I shrug my shoulders.

CHAPTER 8

Serena

"She doesn't like me, and I don't know why. To be honest, I don't really care because she's not really someone I'd be friends with any way, but it is a bit annoying that she's just decided not to like me for no reason," I say.

"What makes you think she doesn't like you?" Brook asks.

"Oh, she made it pretty clear when she was giving me a tour of the building," I say. "It might not be personal though. She might just be a mean girl type who is like that with everyone."

"Or maybe it's not so much that she doesn't like you, but that she was busy and had to work over to get her own work done after taking time out to give you a tour," Brook says. I glare at her, and she laughs and holds her hands up. "I'm not taking this bitch's side. I'm just playing devil's advocate."

"It wasn't just that," I say. "I know it sounds stupid, but when I first went into my office, one of the cables was loose on my computer. I fixed that and then I didn't have any logins. I went down to IT – hence how I met Adam – and got that sorted. Later on in the day, Ruth came to see how I was getting on."

"Well, there you go. She wouldn't have done that if she didn't like you would she?" Brook says.

"Wyatt told her to," I say. "He was out in meetings all day, so he asked her to check in on me with it being my first day."

"Oh, ok. Carry on then," Brook says.

I think for a moment. Where was I? Oh yes. Ruth coming to check in on me.

"So yes. Ruth came to check on me, and she seemed surprised to see that I had my computer up and running. I told her I'd been down to IT, and she got a bit snotty, asking how I knew that was what I was supposed to do. I just shrugged it off and said I thought it was obvious to go to IT for issues with IT stuff. But I swear she looked angry for a moment when she saw me set up. And yes, disappointed. I think she sabotaged me, and she wanted to come back and find me doing nothing because I couldn't login. And then I think she would have told Wyatt that I was useless," I say.

"That's quite a leap Serena," Brook says.

"I know," I say. "And it could be that I am being paranoid, but I'm going to keep my eye on her all the same."

"Oh yeah, definitely watch her. And keep one step ahead of her like today. Like anything you suspect her of doing, don't let on until you're certain. In fact, don't even mention anything happened and she will think all her hard work was in vain and you're not even noticing her inconveniencing you," Brook says with a wicked looking grin.

"Yeah, I plan to keep a close eye on her and ignore her at the same time. Hopefully she'll get bored and go bother someone else," I say.

I have a feeling shaking Ruth off will be a lot harder than that but what the hell. I'm willing to give it a go. And I do quite like the idea of just getting around her little sabotages and pretending I didn't even notice them. I can picture her angry expression and I grin to myself. Bring hated by Ruth for no reason might actually be more fun than I had initially imagined it would be.

CHAPTER 9
Serena

I sit down and have one more read over my presentation. In between working alongside Wyatt on things for his clients, I've been working on everything for Hislop's for almost two weeks now and I know it pretty much word for word but I'm not going to miss an opportunity to have one more read through it and tighten up anything that still needs it. I finish my read through and nothing has jumped out at me as needing changing and for the first time since I started working on this account, I am satisfied that the presentation is as good as it possibly can be.

I already know my branding work is on point and the actual content of the ad pieces for social media and even the TV ad, and normally, once I have those nailed, the presentation pretty much writes itself, but this time it has been a little bit different because of the vegetarian angle. That really has made this whole thing much harder than I thought it was going to be, but I got there in the end and if the client doesn't like it, then they might have to give me some direction about what research they have done on this, and I can incorporate that into the advertising campaign.

I have done so much research on the idea of vegetarianism in dogs, even down to calling a couple of vet practices and I have found nothing and no one to support it being a good idea. In fact, all of the vets I spoke to sounded horrified at the very idea of it. I didn't want to outright lie on the presentation because it would be too easy for potential consumers to check up on the facts for themselves, and so I had to find creative ways to bring in the vegetarianism. I mostly tried to come at it from an environmental viewpoint and I talked a little bit about the vitamins and other good things found in plant-based foods. All true, but still not good for the dogs and I was very careful not to say that it is.

After I finish my last read through of my presentation, I have about fifteen minutes until the presentation is due to start. I have already transferred all the slides and everything to my laptop from the desktop computer and I have triple checked that they are all there and all in the right order. With this done, it should just be a matter of plugging my laptop into the projector and my screen should be presented on the main screen in the conference room, but I want to make sure that I am there in plenty of time to get set up without getting flustered, so I close the laptop and pick it up along with my note book and a pen, and with a deep breath for luck, I leave my office and head downstairs.

I go to the conference room I've been directed to go to, and I get my laptop all set up in under three minutes. I busy myself filling the refreshment jugs; one with water and one with tea. I add lots of ice to both of them, because it is kind of hot in the conference room. I leave them out on the main table with a pile of cups. I'm debating adding some snacks to the table when the door opens, and Wyatt comes in.

I feel my stomach roll deliciously at the sight of him, but I won't let him distract me from my presentation. This is by far the biggest moment of my career so far and I am not going to ruin it by stuttering and spluttering my way through it because the guy I am into is in the room. I'm not sixteen anymore, although it seems I still have the same taste in men as sixteen-year-old me did.

"You're ready," Wyatt says with a smile when he looks around and sees everything set up and the refreshments already out.

"I know," I say. "I just had visions of the projector not working or the cable being missing or one of a hundred other things that could have gone wrong, and me getting all flustered in front of the client, so I got here early. As it turns out, too early because I did refreshments too and it's still a few minutes early."

Wyatt smiles at me.

"It's always best to be prepared," he says. "But you have nothing to worry about. You've got this."

"Thank you," I say, returning his smile with a small one of my own.

Wyatt sits down at the head of the conference room table and pours himself a cup of water. I pour myself a cup of water in case my throat gets too dry and then I go and sit at the opposite end of the room to Wyatt where my laptop is.

Slowly, the rest of the people for the presentation start to show up and as the door closes for one final time, Wyatt smiles and nods to me.

"That's everyone here Serena," he says. "You can begin whenever you are ready."

I wipe the palms of my sweaty hands on the sides of my black dress. I'm pleased that I wore this dress today. It is mostly black – the bodice and the sleeves fully black. Just above the waist, it tucks in and then flairs out into a knee length skirt. Around the bottom of the dress is a white silhouette of various types of flowers. It's one of my favorites of the new dresses and things I bought for work last weekend.

I debated wearing another of my boring pant suits today in case I got too self-conscious standing up in front of strangers with a dress on, but I've mostly stopped wearing those now, opting instead for skirts and dresses. The old pant suit look really isn't the aesthetic here and I want to fit in.

I take a deep breath and let it out in a shaky sigh, and then I stand up and smile at the gathered men and women. I have no idea who is who, not even who works here and who works for Hislop's except of course for Wyatt.

"Good afternoon," I say, smiling ay everyone in turn. "My name is Serena West and I have put together the following campaign for Hislop's, the newest dog food brand on the market. I will take you through the company mission and the branding, the logo, the ads, and the message we want their ideal consumers to hear. When I have finished, I will open the floor up for questions."

I smile and I relax slightly when I see a few of the people smiling, including Wyatt who is nodding his head as well as smiling. It's good to see him pleased and encouraging me to continue. It always helps to know your boss is on board with what you are saying.

I look down at my laptop and bring up the first slide of my presentation. This slide talks about how a plant-based diet is good for your hair and skin and how you get vitamins and minerals you might be missing out on. I then tie that to dogs, including the fact that dogs can't tell us if they have no energy anymore, so we might miss vital signs about their vitamin intake.

I'm about halfway down my speech for this page when Wyatt speaks up.

"Serena, wait a minute," he says. I stop talking immediately. "I know you said questions at the end, but I need to know now. Why are you talking about plant-based diets and their few scant advantages?"

"Well, umm," I start. I clear my throat and start again. "I know it's unconventional when it comes to dog food, but the client's USP is being a vegetarian food and I'll be honest, I struggled to find much of anything that wasn't negative." I shrug my shoulders apologetically. It's not like I didn't try. I spent hours researching this. The Hislop's people must know there is very little information out there. It's not like I am dissing their brand, I'm just stating a fact.

"Wait. You think Hislop's, the company whose branding you have worked on for almost the last two weeks, is making vegetarian dog food?" Wyatt says, looking at me incredulously. I can only nod. I am too afraid to even speak at this point, because I feel like I've made a terrible mistake, but I don't know where or how. "No. Hislop's USP is using sixty percent meat in each of their tins or trays, which is a lot higher than the national average. That's what sets the brand apart and makes it gourmet."

He looks at me in disgust one more time and then he changes his focus to the other people present, his expression changing to one of regret.

"Guys, I am so sorry about this. I must ask you to leave and come back next week if we get this pulled together properly by then. I will send you all the details." Wyatt says.

The others mutter agreement and leave and after a few minutes, there is only Wyatt and me left in the room.

CHAPTER 10

Serena

"You can think yourself very lucky that this was a trial run and you only embarrassed yourself and me in front of company employees. If the Hislop's reps had been here, I guarantee you would have lost us a client and been fired," Wyatt shouts.

I don't know what to say except that I'm sorry, and I really am sorry, but that doesn't seem like it will be enough. I am just about keeping myself from bursting into tears, so I keep quiet for the moment and just let Wyatt fume in his anger. I would be doing the same thing myself in his position. Vegetarian dog food. As if that was ever going to be a thing. I knew it felt off. I should have clarified it. Why the hell didn't I check with Wyatt or someone on his team?

"Go and fix this shit," Wyatt shouts. "And we'll try again tomorrow. Don't let me down again."

I realize he is letting me off the hook, giving me a second chance instead of firing me and I force myself to meet his glare.

"I'm sorry. I won't let you down again," I say.

Wyatt nods once in acknowledgement and then he turns and leaves the room without another word or a glance back. I feel the tears threatening again and I blink them away. I was the one who asked Wyatt to keep it quiet that we know each other because I don't like to mix work with outside of work, and yet I know fine well if my boss who was only my boss shouted at me because I fucked up at work, I would be disappointed in myself, but I certainly wouldn't be on the verge of tears about it.

I take a moment to make sure I'm not going to cry and then I get up and leave the conference room and head back to my office.

I'm shaking as I slam the door behind me and go to my desk and pick up my cell phone. I scroll through my contacts, find Brook's name and hit call. It rings twice before Brook answers.

"Hey," she says.

"She's a fucking cunt," I say. "You know I hate that word but that's what she is. A horrible, backstabbing vile one of those."

"Well, that's some greeting," Brook says. "Who is and what has she done?"

"Ruth," I say. "Remember I told you I had a feeling she sabotaged me with the IT thing?" Brook makes an mm hm sound and then I go on. "Well, I'm certain she sabotaged me this time. Not only did she make me look like the world's stupidest person, but I actually could have lost my job over this."

"Holy shit, what did she do?" Brook demands.

"My dog food campaign. She told me the USP of the product was that it was vegetarian. I couldn't find anything in the brief that hinted at that, and it felt wrong, but I didn't listen to my gut, and I believed her. The company's actual USP is that they have more meat than any current leading brand. I pitched the vegetarian dog food Brook. To what I thought were people from the company. Luckily Wyatt wanted me to have a practice run and they were ad executives from this company but that's bad enough," I say. "Wyatt went ape shit. I didn't tell him Ruth specifically told me the food was vegetarian. Should I have?"

"No," Brook says after a moment. "Not unless it was in an email or something and you could prove it. And when she comes in all smug and asks how it went, because she will, just make on that it went well."

"Wyatt might tell her I'm still working on it," I say.

"Ok, fair point. Tell her that you're making a few adjustments. You don't' have to say what. She'll be expecting you to go mad and accuse her of leading you down the wrong path and then her denying it. Remember, just act like you haven't even noticed she's sabotaging you," Brook says.

"Ok, I can do that," I say.

"Oh, and if you get the chance, offer to grab everyone some coffee and give the bitch a friendly but sarcastic nod," Brook says.

I laugh and nod.

"I might just do that," I say. "Right, I'd best get back to work, I just needed to get that off my chest."

"OK, catch you later," Brook says.

"Bye," I reply.

I feel a lot calmer after my conversation with Brook. Yes, I got yelled at, but that's it. I can fix the pitch easily enough, and now I know for sure that bitch is out to get me so I will be watching my back even more closely.

I sit down at my desk and open my laptop. I decide to work on the laptop rather than my desktop. I lean down and get the adapter out of the bottom drawer and plug it in to the socket and then into my laptop.

I open the presentation, shaking my head at my own

damned stupidity. It was my mistake to continue with the work knowing that the message felt totally wrong – I should have gone and checked it with Wyatt at some point – but although I had played dumb in the conference room, I knew exactly who had set me up: the wonderful Ruth. She had been the one to tell me the brand's USP was being a vegetarian brand and I know I hadn't misunderstood that because it stood out as so weird to me that I clarified it more than once with her and she agreed that I was right about it being weird.

I have no idea why she wants to sabotage me or make me look stupid, but from now on, I won't be trusting a damned thing she tells me that's for sure. If I had only been presenting the work to Wyatt, or Ruth and Wyatt, I could maybe believe it was some sort of jokey initiation thing that all the newbies got, but no way would Ruth do that knowing there was going to be other people in the meeting because it wasn't just me who looked stupid, it was Wyatt as well, because if it was some sort of jokey initiation thing, then surely Wyatt would be in on it, and there was no way he thought anything that happened back there was funny.

I decide that I need to let this go or I will spend hours dwelling on it and still be no further forward with fixing my work. I turn my attention to the laptop. The first thing I do is fix the logo and packaging for the food, both of which are easy fixes as I don't have any of the ingredients lists or nutritional information yet anyway, all I have to do is remove the part where I have said the food is one hundred percent vegetarian and change it to sixty percent meat, which is three times the market average.

Next, I start on all the social media blasts and ads. They take a little bit longer because there are so many of them, but there is nothing difficult to it – again it's really just a matter of switching out one USP for another, because ultimately, my strongest message before I knew I had to switch was that your dog deserves the best and Hislop's is the best. I can still run with that, and I don't even need to skirt around the truth now, because the more meat, the better in this scenario.

I have almost finished tweaking the social media blasts when there's a knock on my office door.

"Come in," I call.

The door opens and Ruth comes in.

CHAPTER 11
Serena

S he smiles widely at me.

"Hi. Sorry I haven't been by sooner, I've been so busy," she says. "I just came to see how the presentation went today."

I almost laugh because this is exactly what Brook said she would do. I remind myself of our conversation and of the fact that I am not going to give her the satisfaction of mentioning what really happened or anything about the vegetarian thing.

"It went really well thanks," I say, with a smile that I hope doesn't look too forced. "There were one or two tweaks requested but like you said before, that's normal."

As I speak, I watch Ruth closely. Her smile slips for the shortest of seconds, replaced by a frown. It could be a frown of confusion because she knows I would have gotten into major trouble for this, or it could have been a frown of anger because she knows I am onto her. I don't care either way. It confirms what I thought I knew; Ruth didn't make any sort of mistake – she wanted to sabotage me. But why? Her smile reappears so quickly it would have been easy to tell myself it never slipped off at all if it wasn't for the other evidence of Ruth's actions towards me.

"That's good then," Ruth says in a voice that tells me that actually she thinks that this is anything but good.

I debate pointing out that she was wrong about the vegetarian angle (wrong but purposely wrong), but I don't. She will obviously deny knowing anything about that and when it gets back to Wyatt which it inevitably will, it will make me look petty as well as mistaken.

"Yes, I thought so," I say. I beam at her. "Thank you for your help."

"Anytime," Ruth says. "And if you need a pair of eyes on the new pitch, let me know."

"I'm pretty sure I've got this, but thank you though," I say.

Ruth nods to me and leaves my office and for the first time since I delivered my incorrect pitch, I feel happy. It's partly because Ruth didn't get the satisfaction of hearing how her sabotage really went and it is also partly because now that I know for definite where the misinformation is coming from, I can check anything too far out there with Wyatt.

I have no intention of taking this matter to Wyatt and getting embroiled in a she said she said argument, especially not with Wyatt's number one trusted employee. If I can catch her in a lie or trip her up somehow though, I can go back to just enjoying my role without having to watch my back all of time. In the meantime, I will be watching my back though, even though I don't think she will try and pull anything for a while now that she knows I'm onto her. And she knows she failed. Or at least she thinks she did, and I can't see her going and asking Wyatt how I did on the presentation, because if she does, it will remind him that she was meant to be checking in on me and keeping me on track, and that will make him stop and think. I still don't think he would assume Ruth was sabo-taging me, but I think he would want to know how the hell she missed that this was a big fuck up.

Once Ruth leaves my office, I get back on with my work and I'm almost finished when my stomach starts growling and I realize how hungry I am. Now that I have noticed, it is a major distraction and I decide to pop along to the kitchen and get something to eat if there is anything left in the fridge at this time of the night. If not, I'm pretty sure there's a Seven Eleven just down the block and it's only getting towards ten – I have plenty of time to get to the store and grab a sandwich or some-thing. I get up and grab my handbag and leave my office. I have only gone two steps when I hear Wyatt calling my name. I freeze. Am I in even more trouble? He might think I'm leaving before I have completed my task, but surely if I explain to him that I was only going to grab some food and come back he will be ok about that. I can't see him objecting to me taking a break and there's no reason for him to think I am lying. Still though, the nerves churn in my stomach.

I force myself to turn to look at Wyatt and I give him a shaky smile. I don't think I've done anything to get me in trouble and I have to act normal until I know what exactly he wants. He closes the gap between us before he speaks.

CHAPTER 12

Serena

"What are you doing Serena?" he asks.

"I was just going to pop out and grab something to eat," I say. "But if it's a problem, I can wait."

"No, it's not a problem. I meant why are you still here at this time?" Wyatt asks.

Oh. So, I'm not in trouble then. Well, that's something at least.

"I just wanted to get the Hislop account fixed," I say. "But I was starving so I thought I'd go and find something to eat and then come back and finish up. I've got about an hour's worth of work left to do and then it's all fixed."

Wyatt shakes his head and my heart sinks. I have done something wrong after all.

"No. There's not a chance you're coming back here tonight," Wyatt says.

"But I need to finish my presentation and get ready for tomorrow," I point out.

"You said you only had an hour's worth of work to do on it, right?" Wyatt says. I nod and he smiles at me. "So, there you

58

go. Finish it up in the morning. And in the meantime, I'm going to take you for dinner."

"Oh no, honestly, it's fine. I'll grab something on the way home," I say. "Thank you for the offer though."

"Serena, it wasn't a request," Wyatt says. "I'm telling you I'm buying you dinner. Now do you need anything else, or do you have everything?"

"I have everything," I say, deciding against arguing the point anymore. I feel like Wyatt offering to buy me dinner is his way of telling me he's over my massive mistake and I don't want to throw the gesture back in his face and have him be pissed off with me again. Plus, I'll admit it. I like the idea of spending some time with Wyatt outside of the office and without my family around. I know nothing can happen between us, but it won't hurt to get to know Wyatt a bit better, and I think it's ok for me to look at him and want him. As long as I don't let him know that I want him. I mean I have been doing that since my teens and nothing bad has ever come of it.

"Then let's go," Wyatt says.

He motions to me to walk slightly in front of him and so I do. We reach the elevators and I press the call button. We don't have long to wait before there's a ping sound and the doors open. I step into the elevator followed by Wyatt, and I press the button for the ground floor. He reaches for it at the same time as I do and for a second, our fingers touch and I feel my skin come alive where he is touching it. I feel him jerk away and I figure for that to be his reaction, he had to have felt that too.

I suddenly feel the air around me change and it's so intense I can almost taste the sex in the air. I know in that moment that this attraction I feel for Wyatt is not one sided as I had always assumed it was. The elevator car reaches the ground floor, and the doors open, and I step out into the lobby. Instantly, that sexual tension I felt in the elevator is gone and as I glance at Wyatt walking along beside me, as casual as ever, I start to think that I must have imagined it all together. Did I really like Wyatt that much that I was starting to imagine a world where he felt the same way? Was I going slightly crazy? Probably not, it was probably just a harmless fantasy, but I definitely think I imagined it.

By the time we get into Wyatt's car, and nothing feels charged or weird, I am certain that I imagined that chemistry between us, that I imagined the idea of Wyatt feeling the same as I do. I am a little bit gutted about that, but I am relieved that I didn't do anything stupid like act on the feeling in the elevator. It was probably nothing more than a blast of static electricity as our hands touched, a perfectly normal reaction, and Wyatt 's pulling away was simply because he didn't like the electric shock sensation. That definitely made a lot more sense.

"Is Italian ok with you?" Wyatt asks as he pulls out of the parking lot and joins the few cars on the road. "There's a great little place not that far from here and I think at this time, they'll be able to fit us in without a reservation."

"Italian is fine," I say. "It's better than fine. It's actually one of my favorites."

"Then you'll love this place," Wyatt says. "It's a little family run place, with real authentic cooking done by Rosa, one of the owners. Guiseppe, her husband and business partner, is the maitre'd and the face of the place, but Rosa's cooking is the heart of the business."

"It sounds great," I say, smiling at the passion Wyatt speaks with when he talks about the restaurant. The food must be really good for him to react like that about it and I'm looking forward to eating there.

My stomach growls at the thought of the authentic Italian food on offer and Wyatt and I both laugh.

"That's your fault," I say, still laughing. "Talking about the place like that and reminding me of how hungry I am."

Wyatt wasn't exaggerating when he said the place was close by. Two or three blocks from the office, he pulls off the main street and onto a smaller side street. About halfway down it, he pulls the car in towards the sidewalk and kills the engine.

"Here we are," he says.

We both get out of the car, and he points to the restaurant's entry way, a black, fancy wrought iron gate is pulled shut across the deep red door. I genuinely think I would have missed it if Wyatt hadn't known exactly where it was.

"Do we need to knock or something?" I ask.

Wyatt shakes his head.

"No, just push the door," he says.

I do and I realize that the wrought iron gate is just painted on the door. It is done exceptionally well, and I never would have guessed it wasn't real. I smile as I step inside of the restaurant. It's small enough to feel intimate but not small enough to be awkward. The tables are set far enough apart that there is privacy, and each table has a small candle burning in the center. The tables are all wooden as are the chairs, although the seat part of the chairs is cushioned with red and burnt orange colored seating squares.

The walls are decorated in reds, oranges and yellows and the lighting is low. The floor is bare concrete, and it is immaculate as is the whole place. There are two or three other couples eating but there are plenty of empty tables and I think Wyatt was probably right about them being able to fit us in without a reservation.

The air smells of garlic and roasting meat and I am embarrassed when my stomach growls again at the delicious smell and Wyatt laughs quietly. Before he can tease me about it, a door opens, bringing the smell of cooking food even more intensely to the room and I can feel my mouth watering.

The man who has appeared through the door looks like he is in his mid-fifties. He's wearing black pants and a black tie and a white shirt. His black hair is neatly gelled back, and his shoes are so shiny I feel like I would be able to use them as a mirror. His caramel skin is lined around his eyes, but the warmth of his brown eyes makes me think those lines are genuine laughter lines rather than wrinkles.

I get further evidence of this when the man beams at us and his whole face lights up. He extends a hand to Wyatt who takes it. The man pumps his hand up and down twice and then pulls him in for a hug, before turning his attention to me. He takes hold of my shoulders and air kisses my cheeks one then the other and finally, the first one again.

"Wyatt, how good to see you," the man says in a heavily accented voice. "How are you? And who is this?"

"I'm good thanks Guiseppe," Wyatt says with a smile. "This is my friend and colleague, Serena West."

"A pleasure Miss West," Guiseppe says, taking my hand in his and kissing the back of it.

"Oh please, call me Serena," I say.

"Serena. A beautiful name for a beautiful young lady," Guiseppe says.

It would have sounded cheesy from anyone else, but somehow, from Guiseppe it sounds like a genuine compliment, and I smile at him, feeling my cheeks turning pink at his words.

"Any chance of a table for two Guiseppe?" Wyatt asks. "We won't keep you late, I promise."

"A table for two? Si. Si," Guiseppe says. "You are welcome to stay as long as you would like to."

He turns away and beckons for us to follow him. He leads

us to a table between the bar and the front window. It's an ideal spot for people watching and it's as far from the other diners as he could get us without putting us in the kitchen. It's a good choice from someone who isn't sure about the dynamics here. It could be seen as a private spot if we were on a date, but as friends, it could also be seen as a prime spot due to being so close to the window. Guiseppe clearly knows his business well.

CHAPTER 13

Serena

"Is this ok for you?" Guiseppe asks and both Wyatt and I nod our heads.

Guiseppe pulls out a chair and gestures for me to sit. I smile at him and sit down, and he tucks me in under the table.

"Thank you," I say, pleased that he has chosen the seat with the best view of the window for me.

"You're welcome. Ricardo will be along any moment with your menus. Can I take your drinks order?" Guiseppe said.

"I'll have a soda and lime please," Wyatt says, and all eyes are on me.

I debate getting a soda too. Wyatt is my boss after all, but we're not in the office and it's certainly not work hours and I think fuck it.

"Can I have a small white wine please?" I ask. "The house white is fine."

"Of course," Guiseppe says, and he moves away from the table.

"Aww he's lovely," I say when he's out of ear shot.

"He is," Wyatt agrees. "He has so much energy and nothing is ever too much trouble for him. Rosa is the same."

"You must come here a lot," I say. "For you all to be on first name terms I mean."

"I do come here quite a lot," Wyatt says. "I often grab a takeout even if I don't want to dine in. But the funny thing is, we were on first name terms within minutes of me coming in the door the first time I came here. That's just the sort of place it is. By the time I left that night, I felt like I was a part of their family. Of course, they'll keep their distance more tonight."

"Why is that?" I ask.

"Because they don't know for sure whether we're on a date or not and they won't want to intrude. The first time I came here, I was with my parents and my sister so there was none of that," Wyatt explains.

I feel my cheeks turning pink again and I smile. I don't really know what to say and when someone who I assume is Ricardo comes to our table with our drinks and our menus, I'm so relieved I could hug him.

He puts the drinks down in front of us and we both thank him, and then he gives us a menu each and again, we both thank him.

"Everything sounds lovely," I say after I've looked over the menu and I glance up to find Wyatt sitting with his menu closed in front of him. "Have you chosen already?"

He smiles and nods.

"You can't beat the classic Cozze alla Tarantina," he says. I must look as confused as I feel because he laughs softly and translates for me. "Mussels with linguine in a red wine sauce."

"Say, that does sound good, but I'm not big on seafood," I say. "I try to avoid anything that is served to me with a face or with a shell."

Wyatt laughs softly and I join him.

"I'm going to go with a classic I reckon," I say after studying the menu for a little bit longer. "Lasagna."

"Good choice," Wyatt says, and when our waiter comes back to see if we are ready to order yet or not, Wyatt gives him both of our orders.

"So, what made you want to work in marketing?" Wyatt asks as we wait for our food to be brought out to us.

"Funnily enough I never even considered marketing as a career opportunity until after I started college," I tell him. "When I left high school, I knew I wanted to go on to college, ideally an ivy league school. The thing was I didn't really know what I wanted to do after that, so I had some trouble choosing a degree. I talked to my dad, and he said if I had a passion, I should follow that, and if I didn't, then I should study business in general, because once you know how a business works, that will open a lot of doors for you. I took his advice and took the management and marketing course. Somewhere along the line, I realized I had fallen in love with marketing, and even further down the line, I realized I was damned good at it too."

Wyatt smiles at me and I feel my cheeks turning pink again under his stare.

"It's a good feeling, isn't it? The moment you realize what you are meant to do with your life," he says.

"Yeah, it really is," I say. At that moment the waiter arrives. He puts my lasagna down and then Wyatt's mussels and pasta. "This feeling beats it though. When you are so hungry and are given food."

"I'll second that," Wyatt laughs.

For a while we fall silent while we eat.

"This is so good," I say after a while. "How is yours?"

"Amazing," Wyatt replies.

I pick up my wine glass and take a sip. I can feel Wyatt's eyes on me, and I look up and catch his eye and hold it while I have another sip of wine and then I set the glass down. I'm tempted to reach out and touch his hand, but I stop myself. It's one thing looking at him for a moment too long but touching him wouldn't be so easy to explain away if he didn't appreciate it.

"Would you like another glass of wine?" Wyatt asks and I'm surprised when I look down and see mine is nearly empty.

I shaky my head.

"I'd better not, thank you," I say.

I'd love another one. In fact, I'd quite like to get drunk with Wyatt because I'm sure if we did that, we'd be a lot less cautious around each other, but Wyatt is only drinking soda and there's no way I'm going to embarrass myself while he's stone cold sober.

"Are you sure?" he presses, as I take my last mouthful of my lasagna. I nod. "OK, then how about a coffee with dessert?"

"I don't think I can eat dessert," I say, sitting back in my chair and rubbing my full stomach.

Wyatt shakes his head and laughs.

"There is always room for gelato Serena," he says, his tone of voice mock serious but his expression teasing.

I love the way he sounds when he says my name and I find myself agreeing to the gelato. God am I really that easily swayed? A sexy voice says my name and I'm his? There's a bit more to it with us than that though. And let's be honest here, his theory isn't wrong. There really is always room for gelato.

Our waiter comes over with a bowl of strawberry gelato for me and chocolate gelato for Wyatt, plus two coffees. We each try our gelato and it is amazing.

"Oh wow," I moan. "That is by far the best gelato I have ever tasted."

"I told you it was a good place," Wyatt says. "But you're only partly right. The chocolate is better than the strawberry."

"No way," I say.

Wyatt puts some chocolate gelato on his spoon and holds it out to me. I take it and try the chocolate gelato and he's right, it is damned good, but I still think I prefer the strawberry. I hold out my spoon loaded with the strawberry gelato and instead of taking the spoon, Wyatt moves closer to me and eat the gelato off the spoon with me still holding it. I feel my pussy clench as he looks into my eyes as he swallows.

"Ok, let's compromise. They are both better than literally anywhere else," Wyatt says.

I squirm slightly in my chair, not sure if I want to take the pressure of my pulsing clit or whether I want to press down on it harder, and I smile and nod.

"Deal," I say.

We chat while we finish up our gelato and coffee. When I finish my coffee, I am more than satisfied, but I'm really enjoying Wyatt 's company and I don't want the night to end, so when he asks if I fancy one more, I happily agree. We are getting flirty, there's no denying that, but he's also making me laugh, and when my hand touches his as I put my cup down on the table, he doesn't move his hand away and I don't either.

CHAPTER 14
Serena

We are on dangerous ground, but I don't care. I've wanted Wyatt for so long and now he's starting to act as though he might feel the same way as I do, I am not going to run from this. I pick my coffee back up with my other hand so that I still don't have to move the hand that has contact with Wyatt 's hand. I sip my coffee and look around, and as much as I don't want to break the spell, I know I have to speak up.

"Wyatt, we're the only ones left in here," I say. "I think they're waiting to close."

Wyatt looks around and makes a face at me that says he feels guilty. He waves at the waiter and asks him for the bill. As we wait for the bill, Guiseppe comes over and asks us if everything was ok with our food. We both gush over how amazing it was and Guiseppe's face lights up.

"I'm sorry we overstayed our welcome," Wyatt says. "I promised you we wouldn't do that and yet here we are."

"Nonsense," Guiseppe says, waving away Wyatt's apology. "You could not overstay your welcome here because you are always welcome."

He squeezes my shoulder and then Wyatt's and then he moves away as Ricardo comes back with the bill. Wyatt takes it and then he takes a small handful of bills from his wallet and leaves them with the bill, and we get up and head for the door. We call our goodbyes and Ricardo and Guiseppe return them and then we are out in the street and Guiseppe slides the bolt across on the door behind us, turning the little sign from open to closed. I glance at my watch, and I am surprised to see that it's after half past eleven.

"Where abouts do you live?" Wyatt asks me as we walk to his car. I tell him and he raises an eyebrow. "Seriously?"

"Yes, why? Is there something wrong with that area or something?" I ask with a frown.

"No, I'm just surprised that out of the whole city, you live between the office and my place. That's good really though. If it's all the same to you, I'll drop you off at home now and pick you up tomorrow, save going back for your car," he says.

"Yeah sure, that's great," I say.

Does he really mean he's just going to drop me off, or is he hoping I'll invite him in, because that obviously wouldn't happen if we went back for my car. I don't know if that is what he wants, and to be honest, I don't know if I'll be brave enough to ask him in, but I want to. God how I want to.

We are almost at my place, and I'm still debating whether or not I dare invite Wyatt in when it suddenly hits me that I don't have my keys. They are in my jacket pocket and my jacket is still hanging up in my office at work. When I left my office, I was only planning on going to the kitchen or the Seven Eleven and coming straight back and when Wyatt asked me to have dinner with him, I was so flustered that when he asked if I had everything I needed, I just said yes. It was a warm enough night that I didn't need the jacket and I didn't even give my keys a second thought until now.

"Fuck," I say underneath my breath.

"What's up?" Wyatt says, glancing across at me and then turning his attention back to the almost deserted road we are moving along on.

"I've left my keys at work," I tell him sheepishly. "I'm sorry, can we go back to the office?"

He glances at his watch and shakes his head.

"It's after eleven, that'll mean calling the super of the building to let us in. You can just stay at my place," Wyatt says. "If you are ok with that of course."

I feel a tingle go through my body and the hairs on my arms stand up.

"Yeah, that's ok with me," I manage to say.

It confirms that I was right; he was angling for an invite in when he dropped me off, otherwise he would have taken me to the office. People like Wyatt don't worry about calling the super of the building out of hours. It's not like he can get him fired or anything.

I don't want to jump the gun or look like I'm desperate, so I force myself not to sit there grinning like some sort of idiot and instead, I look out of the window as we pass by where he would have turned off to get to my street house. Instead, we keep going and about six blocks later, he turns to the left, the opposite side to my place. The posh side. I guess it stands to reason that the owner of a multi-million-dollar company is going to live on the nicer side than someone who has only been out of college for five minutes and until last week, only had temporary jobs.

He pulls off the street, driving down a ramp into an underground parking lot. He parks and we get out of the car, and he leads me to an elevator. We get in and Wyatt leans across me and hits the button for the top floor. I get a whiff of his aftershave, musky and masculine and I relish the scent. It makes me want to grab Wyatt and kiss him so that I can be consumed by that scent. I force myself to behave like a normal human being instead though.

We go up and up and up and eventually, the elevator comes to a stop and the doors ping open. The apartment building is not quite as posh as I imagined it to be at first because the doors of the elevator don't open into Wyatt's living room.

They open into a short hallway which Wyatt leads me down and then he opens a door and gestures for me to enter. His open plan living room, dining room and kitchen is massive. The wall opposite where we enter is all glass and he has a beautiful view over the city. The skyline is visible with the darkness inside of the apartment and I can see other high rise apartment blocks, some windows lit up, some not. The twinkling lights look almost like stars from here.

"Lights," Wyatt says as he closes the door and the lights pop on, dimmed to just a nice, cosy level, but still enough to cause the window to become more like a mirror and now I see myself and Wyatt reflected in it instead of the city scape. "Let me show you the spare bedroom and where the bathroom is."

Obviously the second part of Wyatt 's sentence is aimed at me, and I nod and follow him across the huge lounge area. He opens a door that opens into a long hallway, and he leads me down it. He opens a door and points inside, commenting that the room is the bathroom as he is showing me it. The bathroom is big too, holding a large double shower, a free-standing bath and several storage units. After I have had a peep inside the bathroom and nodded my acknowledgement of the room, Wyatt opens the door opposite it, and gestures for me to go inside of it, which I do.

"This is my spare room," he says. "Sorry it's not much."

The room has a double bed, made up with black bedding

that matches the curtains. The walls are white and the floor, like the wardrobe and other furniture, is oak. It's plenty big enough and I have no idea what Wyatt means when he apologizes for the room not being much. I wonder how big his bedroom is if this one feels like a room he has to apologize for.

"Is this ok for you?" Wyatt asks me.

"Of course, it's ok for me," I say. "It's more than ok. It's great. Thank you."

I can feel that tension in the air again, although I think I might be imagining it this time, my imagination running loose now that I'm officially standing inside of a bedroom with Wyatt beside me. Is Wyatt about to get into bed with me? I hope so, but I still don't believe it's going to happen.

"Do you want a drink or anything before bed?" Wyatt asks me.

"No thank you," I say.

"Ok, well if you want anything at any point, help yourself. If you want to brush your teeth, there's a spare toothbrush in the cabinet above the bathroom sink," he says. "There are toiletries and everything in the bathroom. Use anything you want to. Oh, and there are towels for you to use right there in the tall cabinet."

He points to a cabinet set into a corner of the room, and I nod again, letting him know I'm listening and that I understand.

"Thank you," I say, the talk of a toothbrush and towels suddenly bringing on the grubby feeling I always have at the end of a long day. The fact that Wyatt is giving me directions for where to find stuff tells me he's not planning on being in here with me. I don't know if I misread the situation earlier or if the moment just passed but the tension is gone, and I'm going to be spending the night in here alone. In that case, I might as well at least be comfortable. "Actually, I was thinking of taking a bath if that's ok. I know it's kind of late, but ..."

I tail off and Wyatt smiles.

"I'm a bit of a night owl myself," he says. "Knock yourself out. I'm going to work out I think."

"What, you're going to the gym now?" I ask.

He laughs softly.

"I have a home gym," he explains.

"Oh, of course," I laugh. "I won't bother getting a bath then because you'll want a shower won't you and I don't want to be a nuisance."

"You're not a nuisance and my shortest work out is over an hour, so you have plenty of time," he says.

"Ok," I say.

I decide I will have that bath after all. Although I would prefer to go along to the gym and be a spectator in there instead. I wonder what Wyatt would do if I went and found his gym and just sat down and started to watch him. I imagine him showing off, flexing his muscles and doing a more intense routine to impress me. Truthfully though, I think he would be more likely to ask me what the hell I am doing there and let's be honest, it would be a fair question.

I wait in the bedroom until I hear that Wyatt has opened and then closed a door, and I figure he is either in his bedroom or the gym now, and I step out into the hallway and go across to the bathroom. I put the plug in the bath and get the hot water going. I go to the sink and open the cabinet and find a new toothbrush exactly where Wyatt said I would. I use some of his toothpaste and brush my teeth and then I rinse my mouth and look at myself in the mirror. I splash water on my face and use my fingers to wash my make up off. I decide I don't want to go to bed with wet hair, and I don't think Wyatt will have a hair dryer and I don't want to disturb him by asking him for one, and so I go back to my room and find a hair tie in my bag. I go back to the bathroom and pull my hair up into a bun on the top of my head.

I add some cold water to my bath water, but not much. Just enough so that I can bear the heat on my skin. I love a hot bath. I add a dash of Wyatt 's bubble bath and then I go back to my room again. I strip off and hang my clothes in the wardrobe, aware that I'm probably going to have to wear them again tomorrow.

I open the bedroom door and glance both ways when I realize that I forgot to bring a towel back to the bedroom with me and I'm going to have to duck across the hallway naked or go and get dressed again and go for a towel. I choose the naked dash.

I look both ways along the hallway again. The coast is clear, and I run across the hallway and back into the bathroom. I giggle to myself about my naked dash as I get into the bath and then I lay back, letting the heat caress my skin. I close my eyes and breath in the scented steam from the bath water. I feel my muscles relax and I embrace the feeling.

I wake up and I have no idea where I am. I'm lying in a pool of cold water and Wyatt is there. He is wearing a pair of shorts and nothing else. His toned body looks amazing, covered in a sheen of moisture and glistening in the light. I want to reach out and touch him, to lick him all over.

"Shit, sorry, I didn't know you were still in here," he says.

He might be sorry but I'm not. I am very much enjoying this view, even if I have no real idea what's going on. Wyatt starts to back off, the door closing behind him.

"Wyatt, wait," I say. He stops and I freeze for a second. I

asked him to wait without thinking because I need to feel his body against mine, need to feel his hands on my skin. I can't say that though. I think quickly and settle for something else. "Where am I? Why am I in a tub of cold water?"

Wyatt stops backing away and stops pulling the door closed. He smiles at me and shakes his head but not in a bad way, in a way that says I am amusing to him.

"You're in the bath. You must have fallen asleep," he says.

I look down and see the thick layer of bubbles coating me and I realize he is right. I'm staying at his place because my keys are stuck in the office, and I vaguely remember getting into a red-hot bath and telling myself I was just going to close my eyes for five minutes. I laugh softly.

"Wow. I must have been out for the count," I say. "This water really is cold."

I sit up and the bubbles start to slide down off me. Wyatt jumps forward and grabs a towel and hands it to me to cover myself. As I reach out to touch it, his hand brushes mine and he sucks air in through his teeth and I know he felt that jolt of desire the same as I did. There's no way he thought that was just static electricity. His reaction said it all. Without giving myself time to over think things and chicken out, I reach up and cup the back of his head, pulling his face down to mine until our lips meet.

For a second, I wonder what Brook would think of this. Would she be proud of me? I mean it wasn't exactly subtle, but I sure let Wyatt know I like him.

For a moment, Wyatt kisses me back and I can taste the salty sweat on his lips from his workout and his tongue pushes against mine and I want him to devour me. All too soon though, Wyatt pulls back from me and shakes his head.

"Shit. Sorry Serena. That ... that shouldn't have happened," he says.

He puts the towel down on the side of the bath and leaves the bathroom without looking back. I can't help but smile to myself. That kiss was every bit as magical as I had hoped it would be, and I might have believed that Wyatt was sorry about it if it wasn't for the fact that I could see his huge hard on through his shorts.

CHAPTER 15
Serena

I get up quickly once I'm alone. I step out of the bath and wrap the towel around me because I really am cold now. I pull the plug and wait impatiently for the water to empty out of the bathtub. Once it does, I rinse it around and then I leave the bathroom. I call out to Wyatt and let him know I'm done. I'm not sure where abouts in the apartment he is, but he answers me, so he has obviously heard me.

I go to my room, and I let the towel fall to the ground and then I pull on the robe I found hanging in the closet and then I get underneath the covers to warm myself through a little bit. I lay there, my mind going to Wyatt and his mouth on mine. Oh, why couldn't he have just let go of his inhibitions and showed me heaven. I bet if he had, I wouldn't be cold now, that's for sure.

At some point, I hear Wyatt going into the bathroom and then I hear the shower going on. A shiver of desire goes through me at the thought of Wyatt being naked and so close to me. Without being conscious of doing it, I open the robe and push it apart. I open my legs and slip my fingers between my lips and rub them back and forth over my clit as I see

Wyatt in my mind's eye, naked, wet and utterly fucking gorgeous.

I keep rubbing myself, enjoying the sensation and the images of Wyatt in my mind. I'm not far from coming when I hear the water shut off. I have more than enough imagination to finish myself off without the sound of the shower running, but I pull my hand away from myself anyway. I have decided that I'm done messing around. Now I know for sure that Wyatt wants me as much as I want him, I am going to hold myself back from orgasming until I can have the real thing. And I am going to do everything in my power to see that it happens tonight.

I ask myself what Brook would do in this situation, and I smile to myself as the answer comes to me. Am I going to dare to do it though? You know what, I really think I am.

I wait for around fifteen agonizing minutes after the water shuts off. I figure that's plenty enough time for Wyatt to get back to the bedroom, dry off, sort anything he wants to sort for tomorrow, and get into bed. I want him in bed comfortable and relaxed when I go to him. I don't want him tense or in the middle of something, so I force myself to wait another few excruciating minutes. I don't want to wait too long and go too far the other way and have Wyatt already be deeply asleep when I go to him.

Finally, I decide that I can't wait any longer. More than enough time has to have passed and I slip out of bed. I keep the robe on, but it won't be on for long. I leave my room and make my way towards Wyatt's room. My stomach is churning in excitement and my body tingles at the thought of what I am about to do. I get to Wyatt's room, and I raise my hand to knock but I decide against it. It will be too easy for Wyatt to ignore a knock and just pretend he was asleep if I question him about it later. I can't just barge in there though – that's too forward and rude. I think for a minute and then I knock on the door and call out at the same time.

"Wyatt? It's me, Serena. Can I come in for a minute please?" I ask.

"Yeah, come on in," Wyatt replies from the other side of the door.

I take a deep breath and let it out slowly and then I open the door and go into the room. Wyatt is on his bed. He is sitting up with the sheet and duvet loosely piled in his lap.

"Are you ok?" he asks as I walk further into the room.

I nod and keep walking. When I'm a few feet away from the bed, I stop walking.

"I can't sleep," I say. "I thought maybe you could help me."

"I don't know how, but if you ..." Wyatt is saying, but he stops talking, presumably in shock, when I reach up and open the robe and then let it slip down my arms and onto the ground.

I watch as Wyatt's pupils widen, his eyes lustful. He bites down on his bottom lip and looks at me and I smile in what I hope is a sexy way. It must have been something like close to right because Wyatt makes a low growling sound in his throat and then he's pushing the covers back and getting to his feet. His workout shorts are gone, and I moan with desire when I see his hard cock.

He closes the gap between us and wraps his arms around my waist, pulling me against him. Our lips meet and we're kissing, and I can feel my skin touching his skin all along the front of my body. I am almost dizzy with desire, and I wrap my arms around Wyatt's shoulders and cling to him as we kiss.

Our kiss is hungry, our tongues probing around, our lips mashed together. It's the sort of kiss I have always imagined sharing with Wyatt and now I am and it's everything I had thought it would be and more. His hands roam over my body, caressing me and tickling me. I hardly dare to move in case it somehow breaks the spell between us, and he walks away from me again.

Our kiss deepens, and our tongues collide and caress each other's. I get brave and press my body against Wyatt's. I can feel his hard cock against me, and I move my hips gently, applying a light pressure to it. Wyatt moans into my mouth and then he pulls back from the kiss and for a horrible moment, I think he's going to say it's over; we're done. But instead, he turns me around so that I am facing away from the bed and then he pushes me gently into a sitting position on the edge of his bed.

He kneels down on the floor in front of me and nudges the insides of my knees with his hands. I know exactly what he wants, and I open myself up to him, spreading my legs wide open and displaying my wet pussy, my swollen clit, and inviting him in. I lean back on my elbows as Wyatt moves in closer to me and begins to work my clit with his tongue. His tongue on me sends bursts of pleasure through my body, but it also leaves me wanting more. For each little burst of pleasure I feel, I am left with a longing for a climax.

He licks and sucks me, pushing me closer and closer towards the anticipated climax and I twist the sheet beneath me into tight little balls in my fisted hands as the sensations become almost too much for me to bare.

Just when I think I can't take this anymore, Wyatt pushes two fingers inside of me. He works the fingers in time with his tongue and although I try to make it last because I am loving the feel of it, I can't hold myself back for long and I succumb to my orgasm.

Every muscle I have clenches at once as pleasure assaults me, spiralling out from my clit and pussy, moving up to my stomach where the muscles there contract deliciously. From there, the pleasure seems to spread like a warm glow through my entire body until every part of me is consumed by this feeling of release, of ultimate animalistic ecstasy. It's pure. It's raw. It's absolutely amazing. It's just ... wow.

I come down slowly, my pussy involuntarily clenching and unclenching as my muscles slowly relax. Wyatt pulls his fingers out of me, but he still keeps licking away at my clit and the lightning bolts of pleasure that go through me now are so intense on my swollen clit that they are almost painful, and I only manage to keep my legs open so wide because Wyatt is between them stopping me from closing them. It's not that I want him to stop, I just think if the space wasn't blocked, closing my legs against the intense feeling would be almost a reflex action.

Growing up, my dad was pretty strict about boys. In fact, no, scratch that. My dad was an absolute tyrant when it came to boys, so much so that me even attempting to date anyone was futile and I just gave up in the end. When I went away to college, that all changed and I had more than my fair share of dates and I suppose you could say that I have had a kind of sexual awakening over those four years, but in all that time, I have never once felt anything like the full body orgasm Wyatt just gave me.

I can finally breath almost normally again and already I am craving that feeling again, even as little bursts of pleasurable pain course through me. Wyatt lifts his head up and I can't help but notice that the bottom half of his face is wet from me. I feel like I should be embarrassed by this, but I'm not. I am happy to own my pleasure and I'm not done with that yet.

I move backwards across the mattress and then I reach out for Wyatt as he half stands up. I pull him down on top of me and he comes with no resistance. His lips find mine again and

I can taste my own orgasm on his lips and on his tongue. I want to make Wyatt feel as good as he made me feel and I reach down between the two of us and wrap my fist around his cock. I roll, pushing Wyatt off me and onto his back and I follow, kneeling between Wyatt's spread legs.

I keep his cock in my fist, and I start to move my fist up and down his length when he lands on his back. He closes his eyes and moans, a low moan so full of desire it sends a shiver through my body and makes me pussy get even wetter. I keep moving my hand, varying the pace and the pressure I put on Wyatt's cock.

One minute I'm holding him firmly, my movements fluid and fast and I can see him hurtling towards his orgasm and so I change it up a bit, slowing the pace completely and using a feather like touch that makes Wyatt moan again, but this time, in frustration. I keep teasing him, bringing him to the edge and then backing off a little bit and leaving him there.

Finally, I realize I'm teasing myself almost as much as I'm teasing Wyatt. I am more than ready to feel his cock inside of me. I release Wyatt's cock from my working fist and his eyes fly open. I smile down at him as I move onto all fours and get my legs on the outside of his so that I am straddling him.

I keep looking down into his eyes as I reach behind me and grab his cock. I hold it still and then I lower myself down onto it. I enjoy watching Wyatt's face as I take him into me. He looks so intense and his mouth twists in pleasure as I take his full length all the way inside of me. I can feel him stretching me out and it feels good to be so full, so entirely consumed by Wyatt.

I lean forward, careful to keep Wyatt inside of me and I kiss his lips gently, running my lips over his, more of a teasing touch than a kiss.

He moans against my lips and the vibrations tickle in a

delicious way. I kiss him hard and fast and then I straighten up and begin to move up and down on his cock. I clench and unclench my pussy as I move, and I can feel every bit of Wyatt's cock as I grip it. I start to move faster, spurred on by Wyatt's moans.

I push my hips forward slightly so that Wyatt's cock rubs over my g spot with each thrust. I feel my bladder contract and I tighten my muscles until the feeling of needing to pee passes. The second thrust feels nice and the third one feels amazing. I keep moving and as I do, I reach up with both hands and caress my breasts. I roll my nipples between my fingers until they are hard little points and then I reach down with one hand and push two fingers into my slit and onto my clit.

My thrusting movement sends my clit over my fingers, and I gasp as the pleasure intensifies. I am so close to coming again and I'm grinding down on my fingers and on Wyatt's cock with an intensity that is almost savage, but I don't care if it is savage, it feels so good, and I have no intention of stopping. I don't think I could stop now even if I wanted to.

Wyatt watches me on top of him, working both of us into a frenzy, my breasts bouncing around on my chest as I move. His eyes are heavy with lust and his mouth is slightly open as he pants for breath. He is thrusting in time with me, his hips working with me, and his thrusts are every bit as hard and as desperate as mine are. I feel better than I can ever remember feeling in my body, my mind and my soul.

My clit gives one last hard thrum of pleasure, and my orgasm explodes and tears through my body. I have to pull my fingers away from myself straight away because my clit is now so tender, I can't bear to touch it anymore.

My orgasm spreads out through my pussy and down my thighs, making my skin there tingle and tickle, like fingernails are running over it on the inside. The pleasure runs up over too, filling my stomach and chest with heat and making the muscles in my stomach tighten.

I'm at the peak of my climax, and I am falling to the side and then I'm on my back and Wyatt is on top of me again as fireworks continue to explode in my stomach and in my clit. My pussy is going wild, moving of its own volition, clenching and squeezing Wyatt's cock, and I can see by the way his face is contorted that he is loving every second of this as much as I am. He thrusts into me, hard and commanding and I am only too happy to let him set the pace. I match him thrust for thrust, clinging to him, and throwing my head back as he kisses my neck, letting him reach the tender skin there easier.

With one final hard thrust into me, Wyatt hits his climax. He holds me in place, his cock pushed so far into me that I can feel it pushing against my cervix. I feel him twitch and then I am filled with a flood of wet heat as he comes hard. He growls my name and then he curses several times and my poor battered clit pulses when I hear my name on his lips like that. No one has ever been able to make me react like that with only their voice before.

Wyatt thrusts into me again and he spurts again and then he slips out of me and rolls off me, leaving me feeling cold and empty without him inside of me anymore. We lay side by side for a moment while we get our breath back. I float down gently as though I'm gliding through feathers and by the time my breathing has evened out and I feel normal again, I am almost asleep. Wyatt's voice pulls me back awake although I would have preferred to just snuggle down and go to sleep, especially when I hear what he has to say.

I roll onto my side to face Wyatt, and he runs his hand over his face.

"Shit Serena, I'm so sorry. I can't believe I let that happen again, I ..." he starts.

CHAPTER 16

Serena

He regrets what happened between us. That much is obvious. I want to cry, and I want to curl up and die of embarrassment all at the same time. There is only one way I can see to get myself out of this without it being embarrassing.

"You don't have to be sorry," I say with a shrug. "Shit happens."

He turns his head and frowns at me, and I laugh softly.

"What? You think I haven't had a one-night stand before?" I ask.

I can't possibly let him think I did this because I thought he liked me too and that maybe it was going to be the start of something special. I can't let him think that I am some daft kid who still has that crush on him that I had when I actually was a daft kid. I can play this off as something I just wanted in the moment too.

In truth, I am still that daft kid as it turns out. And I have only ever had two one-night stands, and this is one of them. The other one was less embarrassing because we both knew going into it that it was only going to be a one-night stand, but the sex was awful. You can't have it all ways, I guess.

"That's the thing Serena. I've never thought about whether or not you've had a one-night stand before, because I've never thought of you in that light before, nor should I. You're my best friend's brother's daughter," Wyatt says.

"But I am also an adult who can make my own decisions," I counter. "Honestly you're acting like you've taken advantage of me or something."

"I kind of feel like I have. You're so young," Wyatt says.

I snort out a laugh.

"I'm twenty-four," I say. "And if it wasn't for you knowing my dad, you would consider that an adult age. It's not like I'm seventeen or something."

Wyatt nods along to my words because he can't argue something he essentially knows is true.

"And if anyone took advantage of anyone tonight, I was the one who came in here and did a strip tease," I say.

"Fuck, that was hot," Wyatt says, and we both laugh a little bit and some of the awkwardness goes out of the room. "Ok, I think I probably overreacted a little bit there, but seriously Serena, you know this can't happen again, right? It's not just about your dad, although I admit that's a big part of it. There's also the fact we work together now."

"Ok, work I understand," I say, and I do. "But I really don't get the big deal with my dad. Do you think I'm going to call him and tell him what we've done, because newsflash, telling my dad about my sex life isn't a thing."

"No, of course not. I just ... I feel like I am somehow breaking his trust. Like if I had a daughter, I would expect her to be around Craig and Martin and be safe, not be like practically violated."

I laugh. I can't help it. He's so dramatic.

"Sorry," I say. "Look I get what you mean, but I think you're making it a bigger deal than it has to be. If you did have a daughter and she had sex with Uncle Craig, you wouldn't think he had taken advantage of her, would you?"

"Of course, I would," he says without a moment of hesitation.

"Then I hope when you have children you have boys," I reply.

"I can't see me ever having children, but if I do, yeah I think you're right," Wyatt says. "Boys I think will make me less grey less quickly."

"Why don't you ever see yourself having children?" I ask, curious about this despite everything else he's saying. "You would be a good dad."

"To boys?" he says with a smile.

"To boys," I clarify.

"There was a time when I was around your age, I thought I would meet Miss Right, get married, have a couple of kids. I feel like I kind of missed my chance now," Wyatt says. "I don't see me ever finding someone now; I only have time for working."

"Well then you'd better change your no sex with employees rule then," I laugh.

Wyatt laughs too and then he takes my hand beneath the covers and squeezes it.

"I really am sorry Serena," he says. "And I want you to know that I'm not saying this can't happen again, because I didn't enjoy it or because I don't want it to."

"It's fine," I say. "Seriously, I didn't expect it to happen again. I hadn't even thought about that. I just wanted you in the moment and I acted on it. That's it. You're massively over thinking this."

I know what I have to do to convince him that I am not in

the least bit into him. I give his hand a quick squeeze back then I free my hand from his, push the covers back and get up. I saunter to where my robe dropped, letting him have a quick view of what he's turning down, and then I pick the robe up and put it on.

"Where are you going?" Wyatt asks, propping himself up on his elbows.

I can see where his hard cock is pressing the sheet up and God, I want to ride him again, but I won't give him the satisfaction of thinking I want him for more than what I've had.

"Back to bed," I say. "Something tells me I'll be able to sleep now."

I leave the room, forcing myself not to look back. When I've pulled the door closed behind me, I let out a shaky breath. I don't know if I'm more upset that Wyatt has made it clear we won't be doing that again, or happier that I made him think that I felt the same way and not that I had some pathetic little crush on him. Oh, and I'm pretty happy about the fact that I think I left him wanting more. Because while his words tell me he doesn't want this, doesn't want me, his cock tells me he's lying.

CHAPTER 17

Serena

When I woke up this morning, the night before came straight back to me. Not only the delicious orgasms, but the conversation that Wyatt and I had after the sex, where we both agreed that the idea of anything else happening between us is very much off the table.

I agreed when Wyatt said what we had done was a mistake, simply so I didn't look like some ditzy schoolgirl with a crush who thinks every kiss leads to a relationship of sorts. I don't for a second think us being together was a mistake though. Something that felt that good can't be wrong, right? Wyatt said we had made a mistake because he was worried about who my dad was. And also, because we work together. The more I think about this, the more I realize that there is still a bit of hope for us yet.

The working together thing was easy – we would simply not mix business and pleasure. The other thing was a little bit harder; I couldn't really change who my dad was. But maybe over time, Wyatt would see that it wasn't my father's choice who I did or didn't date. Because I learned one thing for sure last night. Wyatt can deny wanting me all he likes. He can find a hundred reasons for us not to hook up again. But beneath it all, he wants me every bit as much as I want him, and I reckon if I bide my time, we'll end up having sex again. Maybe more than once.

The car ride to work this morning was surprisingly relaxed. I really expected it to be awkward, but it wasn't. We didn't talk much, but it was a comfortable silence rather than an awkward one and to be honest, I put it down to it being early in the morning rather than anything else.

We didn't appear to be seen arriving at the office together, or if we did, no one has said anything to me about it and I haven't caught anyone whispering or giggling when they think I'm not looking so that's a bonus at least.

I have spent my day so far finishing up the last few bits I had to do from last night and then just going back over my presentation perfecting it and then checking and double checking it. There is about fifteen minutes until the presentation is due to start and I'm happy with my work, and to make me even happier, I have so far today avoided seeing Ruth. All in all, it hasn't been a bad day for me so far and I'm hopeful that I'm going to keep it that way with the new and improved pitch with no mention of fucking vegetarian dogs.

I gather my things together and head back to the same conference room from yesterday. I get everything set up and run through it all. I am happy with it, but I'm still debating running through it all again, just to be on the safe side. As I debate it, the conference room door opens and Ruth walks in. I instantly decide not to go through the presentation with her here – I won't give her the satisfaction of thinking I'm nervous. Instead, I glance up at her and force a smile.

"Good morning, Ruth. How are you?" I ask.

"Fine thank you," Ruth says, her tone icy. The door to the conference room opens again and Wyatt comes in. All at once,

Ruth's whole demeanor towards me changes, and when she speaks again, the icy tone is gone, and she speaks like she's talking to a friend. "What about you? You're not too nervous, are you?"

"No, I'm feeling pretty confident to be honest," I reply, trying my best not to laugh at the obvious change in Ruth.

Wyatt, oblivious to Ruth's change of attitude, greets us both. Ruth manages to look at me without even looking slightly embarrassed about what she's just done. That only makes the urge to laugh even stronger and I force myself to look back down at my notes until I get myself under control.

"Whenever you're ready Serena," Wyatt says.

I look up from my notes and at Wyatt, frowning with confusion.

"Ok," I say, still confused but then the confusion turns to understanding through what I say next. Wyatt no longer trusts me enough to have other people in here until he has heard the pitch himself. "Is it just you two. I thought ...?"

I trail off before I can say anything that gives Ruth a lead in to say something bitchy, although I am a little bit worried that maybe I already have.

"What I saw last time was good except for the one obvious error," Wyatt explains. "And I went through the rest of the pitch afterwards too. The execs that were in here agreed with me, so I didn't feel the need to disturb them again. Think of this as a dress rehearsal and if all goes well, I'll get the client in."

I can't stop myself from smiling as I get up and start my presentation. My first thought, upon learning the execs weren't coming in, was that my pitch last time has been so bad Wyatt wanted to see it himself first in case I embarrassed him in front of his staff. But it seems that actually, the opposite of that was true. Or even if it wasn't, he had made it sound so and I knew that would piss Ruth off for no real reason and I liked that.

I was already pretty confident about the presentation, and Wyatt's words boost my confidence even more and I sail through my pitch, showcasing the various marketing graphics and the brand message. When I've finished the last screen, I smile out at my audience of two.

"Do you have any questions?" I ask.

Wyatt shakes his head which surprises me. I was expecting a whole slew of questions designed not to throw me off my game, but to get me to learn to respond confidently before the representatives of the brand came along and asked me those same questions.

"Honestly Serena, I like to throw a few questions at my guys at this point, things I think the brand will ask, but you have covered everything so well and I genuinely can't think of anything to ask. The brand will probably come up with something I have overlooked so I apologize if you are caught short but that's where we are," Wyatt says. I beam under his praise. He turns to Ruth. "Ruth? Any questions or thoughts?"

"Not really. It was ok – for the second attempt," she says, and I resist the urge to roll my eyes. I am a little bit hurt that Wyatt doesn't say anything about her attitude. I mean I get it – he trusts her opinion – but he must be able to see that was just her being nasty for no reason. Oh well, never mind. She's not the first mean girl I've dealt with, and she probably won't be the last one either.

I begin to disconnect everything, and I'm soon ready to leave. Wyatt and Ruth are still sitting at the table, and I wonder if I am meant to be staying or if they are waiting for me to go so that they can discuss my presentation in greater detail.

"Is that everything you need from me then?" I ask when it becomes clear that no one is saying anything.

"Yes, thank you Serena," Wyatt says. I start to stand up and he speaks again. "Oh actually, there was something. Do you have a second? I have to go in a moment because I have a meeting, so I don't have time to come back up to your office to talk to you."

"Of course," I say, sitting back down.

Wyatt stands up and walks around the back of my chair.

"You should have an email from me," he says.

I open my laptop back up again and go to my email account's inbox and scroll down, and I see the new email from Wyatt. I click it open, and Wyatt leans forward and points to my screen. As he leans in, his chest brushes my shoulder and I get a whiff of his aftershave and simultaneously, my pussy dampens and my cheeks flush. I try to ignore both and focus on what Wyatt is telling me instead of what my body is telling me.

"So that's what I need from you by the end of next week," he says. "Just the priority order has changed. What was number four," – he points again, and I get another whiff of his delicious scent – "is now taking the number one spot. After number four is done, just start from the original number one and work down."

"OK, got it," I say.

"Great, thanks Serena," he says. "Right, I gotta run. See you later ladies."

We both say our goodbyes and Wyatt leaves the room.

"Well, I see you've been officially initiated into the company now then," Ruth says with a grin.

I don't get her angle, but I don't believe for a second that she is trying to make nice or that she's just making conversation with me. I will play along though and see where she's going with this.

"Yeah. My first full marketing campaign," I say. "And an acceptable pitch delivered."

"That's not what I mean," Ruth says, watching me with calculating eyes.

"Then you've lost me," I say, and I actually mean it. I have no idea what she's getting at.

"Oh, come on Serena, we're both women of the world, and we know how these things work. Wyatt likes fresh meat, and the new associates are always – how should I put this? – eager to please him," Ruth says. "They never say no to him. Just like you didn't."

I think about telling Ruth she's way off, but I know she can see the truth on my face, especially the way I blushed when Wyatt touched my shoulder. I could tell her that I find that line of questioning unprofessional and inappropriate, but that's just another way of admitting it. Instead, I decide to turn the tables on her. Maybe that's why she seems to hate me so much because she had sex with Wyatt when she started here and expected more and didn't get it and now, every time he sleeps with an associate, she's a dick to them. It certainly feels like that would be her style.

"And what about you? How eager were you to please Wyatt when you first started working here?" I ask.

"I'm not an associate," Ruth points out.

"No, but your whole job is literally about keeping Wyatt happy," I say.

"Well, yes, I suppose it is. And as you might have seen, I'm very, very good at it," Ruth says.

She stands up as she talks and then she gives me another of those icy cold smiles and she leaves the conference room, leaving me sitting alone at the table. I sigh and close my laptop again, but I don't make a move just yet. I'm sitting thinking about Wyatt and how I'm just another notch on his bed post. I should probably be angry with him but how can I be when it was me who seduced him? Wait. That's right. I seduced him, not the other way around. If anything, he was reluctant to cross that line.

I smile. I think I have just discovered Ruth's problem with me and her weak spot. She is in love with Wyatt. She must have read our body language right and worked out we'd fucked. And she had decided to try and throw a wrench into the works by making me mad with Wyatt so that it would be us over with.

Oh Ruth, if that's the game you want to play, bring it on, but I guarantee you will lose.

I'm whistling to myself when I leave the conference room and head back to my office to work my way through Wyatt's list of tasks for me to complete.

CHAPTER 18

Wyatt

I walk past the front door, not bothering with it, and go around to the side gate. If I knocked on the front door, chances are Craig wouldn't have heard me anyway and even if he had it would have been a nuisance someone having to come and open the door for me when everyone is in the back garden. This way makes it easier for everyone.

"Hi," I call as I come around the corner of the house into the garden.

"Alright, Wyatt's here," Craig says from his spot in front of the barbecue. He's holding a pair of tongs in one hand and a can of beer in the other and he looks like he's in his element. I smile at him and hold a hand up in greeting.

The smell of cooking meat fills the air making me feel hungry all of a sudden. I look around and spot Craig's parents, Norman and Sandra, both of whom wave hello at me. I wave back at them. The garden is pretty full of people, most of whom I recognize, some of whom are good friends and then there are the odd few I don't know. Of course, I spot Serena a mile off. I think that would be the case wherever we were and however many other people were there.

She's wearing a pair of denim short shorts and a white vest top, her hair pinned back with a clip. She steps out of the kitchen door with a glass of wine in one hand and a can of beer in the other. She crosses the garden and hands the can of beer to Martin. I feel kind of uncomfortable seeing Serena here with her family, but what can I do? I can't just turn down invites to my best friend's events for the rest of my life. These guys are Serena's family, but they are also like family to me too. I remind myself that Serena is a consenting adult and what we did wasn't wrong, but it's kind of hard to think of it as ok here. I would feel pretty betrayed if it was the other way around and I would probably think of times when we've been together like this and be annoyed that they could even look me in the eye.

I shake my head, trying to shake off the thoughts. I have to be normal here and at the moment, I'm so awkward I might as well be wearing a neon sign saying I am hiding something. I wander into the kitchen to grab a drink and I come back out with a can of beer and spot a couple of guys who are friends with Craig and me and I go over to join them, grabbing myself a burger on the way over. As much as I want to talk to Serena, I know it's not a good idea in front of everyone – Craig especially knows me well enough to know when I'm into a girl - and I decide to stick to safer ground, at least until everyone is a bit drunker so they won't be as shrewd.

I've just finished my first burger and damn it is so good. The meat is tender and juicy, and the bun is soft and fresh, the sliced cheese providing the perfect level of tang. Food always tastes better to me when it is eaten outside, especially off a barbecue.

I feel a hand on my shoulder, and I turn around, expecting to see Craig and hoping he has another of those delicious burgers for me. It isn't Craig though; it's Martin.

"Alright Wyatt? Are you avoiding me or what?" he says. "I saw you talking to Craig and thought I might be next you know?"

"Ah well Craig has the food," I joke as we shake hands and clap each other on the back. "It's been a while. How are you?"

"Good, good," he says. "How about you? How's your business going?"

"All good," I say. "Busy but I can't complain about that."

"Yeah, it's a good thing, isn't it? Oh, I've been meaning to thank you as well," Martin says.

"Thank me?" I repeat. "For what?"

"Giving Serena a chance," he says. "She's a good kid and she will work her ass for anyone who gives her the chance to, but so many firms just don't get that do they? They want someone just out of college so they're young and trendy, but they also want them to have like forty years of experience."

This sounds familiar enough that I can't help but laugh.

"Yeah, that sounds like a few of our competitors. I believe in giving people a chance," I say. "And she's working out really well."

"And what do her colleagues think about her fancying the boss?" Martin says.

"Excuse me?" I ask.

What the fuck? Has Serena told him we fucked? He laughs and shakes his head.

"Ah don't act like you don't know what I'm talking about. The kid has had a crush on you since she was about six years old," Martin says.

"Yeah, I'm pretty sure she's grown out of it by now," I say, laughing and trying to sound normal.

The trouble was, I didn't even feel like I knew what normal was anymore. How would I have reacted to this if I didn't think Serena was the hottest woman I had ever laid eyes on? Or if we hadn't fucked? Would I laugh about it and encourage it?

"I don't know about that," Martin says with a grin. He half turns towards the house and when he speaks again, he's shouting to Serena on the other side of the garden. "Hey. Serena?"

"Don't embarrass her," I say as she turns around and takes my breath away with her beauty. Martin ignores me.

"Are you still crushing on Wyatt like when you were a teenager?" he asks.

Serena's cheeks flush bright red and I feel my cock stirring in my jeans. She is always hot, but somehow, she's even hotter when she lets herself get all hot and bothered like this.

"Can't you go and see Uncle Craig's tool collection in his shed or something," Serena fires back and we all laugh.

Craig's parents have wandered over after hearing Martin yelling across the garden at Serena, who has also made her way over, no doubt to avoid any more embarrassing shouts.

"Remember when she used to take out that bit of netting I had beneath one of my skirts and make a veil out of it," Sandra says.

"Oh God yes," Martin laughs. "And she would walk herself down the aisle and marry Wyatt."

"You know, she's old enough for you to make an honest woman of her these days Wyatt," Norman puts in.

I don't know what to say to that and I'm glad when Serena speaks up so that I don't have to.

"Oh no Grandad. Wyatt is a nice guy. My dad would probably approve, but now, I want to teach him a lesson. I'm going to go and find a hot biker guy with loads of tattoos and a long criminal record," Serena says.

"I guess compared to that scenario, I might even approve,"

Martin laughs. He looks at me and he's still laughing but I sense the seriousness of the warning beneath the laughter. "And it's not like she's really going to run off with a Hell's Angel so let's not go getting carried away and thinking you have my permission ok pretty boy?"

"Ugh," Serena says. "If anyone is marrying me, it's my permission they need, not yours."

"Oh yeah? Let's remember that when you come to me for the money to pay for it all," Martin says.

"Umm, no, let's not," Serena laughs and everyone joins her and luckily for me, after that, the conversation moves on to less awkward things.

I excuse myself and head back to the kitchen for anther drink. I open the fridge and peer in. I'm driving so I really just want a soda. I spot some Pepsi at the back of the fridge behind the beer and pull a can of it out.

"Very responsible," Serena says from behind me. I can hear the amusement in her voice, and I turn around to face her. "What's wrong? Scared you might say something you shouldn't?"

"No," I say. "I'm driving, that's all."

I open the soda and take a drink.

"I'm sorry about that by the way," she says, nodding towards the sliding door into the garden. "You know what my dad is like. I really didn't think gran and grandad would join in mind you."

"Don't worry," I say. "They just like to embarrass you is all."

"Well, they sure got their way there then," she says with a smile. "They are majorly embarrassing. I seriously think I might just emigrate."

"That's a lot of effort," I smile.

"Yeah," Serena says. She winks at me, and I realize she's a little bit tipsy. "I guess I'll just have to stick with fucking in secret."

She turns and leaves the kitchen before I can respond leaving me standing there open mouthed, my cock starting to go hard. I force myself to think of Craig, of Martin, and any thoughts of me hardening go away instantly. This girl is going to be the death of me I swear it.

I wait for a second and leave the kitchen behind her. She has moved to where Craig's parents are sitting, and I make a conscious decision to go the opposite way and sit with a couple of the guys I know from our college days. After a while, I excuse myself and go back into the house. I go upstairs to use the bathroom. It is locked when I get there, and I wait. The door opens and Serena smiles out at me.

"I hope you're not following me," she says in a flirty tone which makes me think that actually, she hopes that I am following her.

"Of course not," I say. "In case you haven't noticed, I've been trying to keep my distance all afternoon."

"I've noticed," Serena says.

She puts her head down but not before I notice the look of hurt on her face. I feel awful for making her hurt like that, but what can I do? Serena and I could never work out long term and I feel like if we keep giving in to temptation, it's just going to make not being together harder for us both in the long run.

She walks away without another word and without so much as a glance back and it takes everything I have to go into the bathroom and close and lock the door without shouting after her. I use the toilet and as I do, I decide I am going to have one more drink and then get out of here. I've showed my face so no one can think I'm acting weird or anything, but being around Serena in a non-work situation in front of people who know me so well is just asking for trouble, especially now that she's made it clear she still wants me.

CHAPTER 19

Serena

I have always been at my most comfortable when I'm at my Uncle Craig's place. As a kid, he was always the fun uncle, the one who let me eat things I shouldn't have and do things that I probably shouldn't have been doing. I watched my first horror movie with my Uncle Craig at eight years old and I had my first real drink here when I was eighteen. Now I'm an adult and I can do all those things anywhere I want to, my Uncle Craig is like a good friend, and I still love coming over to his place to just kick back and chill.

Except now it's weird because Wyatt is here, and I want him so badly. I mean that was always a factor in my teens. Hot Wyatt would be round, and I would sit and moon over him. But it's different now I'm not a kid anymore and especially now that we've slept together. The good-natured teasing of my family is no longer funny and Wyatt's laughter, like the very idea of us being together is so ridiculous, no longer bounces off me. Now, it hurts. I just want to go home but I can't think of a good reason that won't either get me teased more or won't worry my family. I'll just have to stick it out. At least I have some eye candy.

Even that doesn't last long. After our bathroom encounter, it seems that Wyatt can't wait to get away. It's barely been fifteen minutes since we ran into each other upstairs and he's starting to say his goodbyes.

"Who is she?" Craig says.

"Huh?" Wyatt says, looking confused.

"Whoever you're going on a date with. She must be hot to drag you away from my amazing culinary skills," Craig says with a grin.

Wyatt laughs and shakes his head. Over the next few minutes, he cleverly protests just enough that Craig and my dad and the other guys are all convinced he's going on a date but have no information or anything to back this thought up whatsoever.

The thought of Wyatt on a date with someone else really hurts me, especially when I let myself imagine for a moment that his date is with Ruth. It's like something hot has been poked into my stomach and it's turning, knotting my flesh, and burning it. I feel sick and I have to work to swallow down the large lump that sits in my throat. I know it's stupid because I know Wyatt is only leaving because things with us are so awkward with an audience that knows us both ways too well. And he's definitely not into Ruth. I would be able to tell if he was. I think he's also totally oblivious to the fact that she's in love with him.

Wyatt puts his hand on my shoulder on his way past me and I feel tingles flood down my body. I force myself to smile up at him like I normally would.

"See you on Monday, Serena," Wyatt says.

"Sure will. Have fun," I say.

"She'll be counting down the minutes," my dad says, and I throw him a dirty look which only makes him laugh more.

Damn, I'm hating this stupid barbecue. I should have just

stayed home. But one thing has come out of it. I know now that no matter how much Wyatt might want me, he will never let himself be with me because of who my family is. I also know, by how much even the thought of Wyatt with another woman hurt me, that I am falling for him fast. I have to nip those feelings in the bud before anything can come of them. I'm going to have to try and keep my distance from Wyatt where possible and where it's not possible if we're working on projects together, I'm going to have to learn how to keep things strictly professional, not just on the outside, but on the inside as well. It's not going to be easy, but it's going to be the only way to protect myself from more pain.

I wait a few minutes after Wyatt leaves before I pull my cell phone out, otherwise I know I'll get teased further. My dad will say I am texting Brook about Wyatt, and I will die of embarrassment, partly because it's true. That's exactly what I'm doing.

"Ugh. Wish you were here, x," I write and send the message to Brook.

"Any other Saturday I would have been. You need to have words with your Uncle Craig and make sure he consults us for our schedules before arranging social events lol. How hard is it being around Hot Wyatt and not letting anything slip? X" Brook sends back.

"My dad thought it would be funny to bring up the crush I used to have on Wyatt when I was a kid and the whole family got involved, even my gran and grandad. Talk about embarrassing. I mean I laughed it off but jeez, x," I write back.

"Awkward. What did Wyatt say? X" her next texts read.

"Not much. He just avoided me all day so that was fun, x," I reply.

"Isn't it what you wanted though? Like in front of everyone, X," Brook replies.

"Well, I thought I did, but then it happened, and I hated it and Wyatt left early and my Uncle Craig teased him about having a date and he didn't say yes or no to whether it was true or not, but he said enough to make my Uncle Craig believe he was right. For what it's worth, I don't think he has a date, I think it was just an excuse to get away. But even just the thought of him with someone else, it hurt me in a way I wasn't expecting. I really think this is more than just me liking him, Brook. I am falling for him hard, and he's not interested in anything more than that one night we had, and I don't know what to do other than just be cold to him and keep my distance whenever I can, x."

My text message is like an essay, but I hit send anyway. If I go back through it and shorten it, I will probably chicken out of sending it.

"Of course, he's interested in more. You know for a fact he is. But he's worried about your dad and your Uncle Craig and work and shit. I agree with your tactic though. Just carry on like you haven't got a care in the world and make sure he always sees you laughing and having fun with other people. It will drive him wild, and he won't be able to keep himself away from you, X" Brook sends back.

"Do you really think so? x" I send.

"Yes. And worst-case scenario, if it doesn't work, at least he hasn't seen you moping around after him, X," Brook texts.

That's true I suppose. I feel marginally better after texting Brook, and I send her a thumbs up emoji.

"Ok, I'll try it and let you know how it goes, x," I write and hit send.

"That's my girl, X," Brook texts back and then sends an emoji of a heart.

CHAPTER 20

Serena

I finish talking and smile around the room, being sure to meet everyone's eye for a second or two. I relax a little bit when I see the faces around the conference room table are all smiling back at me. Wyatt looks happy which means the presentation went well in his eyes which is good, and the Hislop guys look happy too. I mean I don't know them well enough to know if they're just being polite or if they genuinely like what I've done, but at least they aren't frowning or laughing. And even if they aren't happy, Wyatt can't only blame me as he was as excited about this pitch as I was, and I do know Wyatt well enough to know by his expression that he thinks I nailed it.

"Does anyone have any questions?" I ask.

One of the executives asks me about the cost of TV ads. I give them a run through of how the pricing works and how the more premium channels charge more money and the difference in the prices in regard to the time slots the ads run in. They go quiet for a moment and then the one who asked the question whispers to the guy next to him.

I feel a little bit worried, and I glance at Wyatt. He doesn't look concerned, and I think maybe his clients do this regularly. I still don't like it though. They finish and look back at me and they're smiling so that's something I suppose. The man who has been doing the talking looks serious again as he nods to the other guy to speak now. I realize, with a note of panic, that the new speaker is Mr Hislop himself.

"Help me understand something please," Mr Hislop says. I nod for him to go on. "The TV ads are where the biggest chunk of our marketing spending will be going if we choose to incorporate it, correct?" I nod again. "And yet, that kind of advertising, while I agree that it reaches millions, maybe even billions of people, it is completely untargeted."

I nod again. In theory, there is a minor bit of targeting based on the kind of show that is on at the time of the ad. For example, for Hislop's, I would recommend they get at least one ad in a show about pet rescue or an animal hospital. Generally speaking, though, there is no real way to target a TV ad.

"So, in your opinion, would it make more sense to not bother with a TV campaign and spend that money across social media and such where we can target who sees it?" he asks.

I pause. What Mr Hislop is saying is definitely where modern thinking marketing firms are going, but Wyatt and I haven't had this discussion and I don't know how he feels about it. Some of the older firms are old school, but I don't think Wyatt would qualify as old school, but there is definitely more money for marketing firms in campaigns where TV ads are included, and I don't know whether I am meant to say yes or no to that question. I decide in the end to answer truthfully and if Wyatt is angry, well so be it. I don't want to start out by lying to a client.

"There are schools of thought for both types of advertising," I say. "And some products are suited to a mass market campaign, for example, soda or cheese, things everyone uses you know? But for more niche products like yours, in all honesty, I think you would get a lot more return on investment for your money by concentrating on targeted online ads. Maybe you can think about TV ads down the line if you diversify the range, but right now, I think your ideal consumer is going to be much easier to reach online."

"Yes. That's our thinking too," Mr Hislop says with a smile, and I feel my panic melt away. At least now if I get in trouble with Wyatt, it's not because I pissed the client off. "So, if we can go ahead with the billboard campaign on the site you suggested by the vets place on Sycamore Street, the print ads in the animal magazine you mentioned, and then outside of that, let's put the TV stuff on hold and add that extra money to our online budget."

"Yes, of course," I respond. "I can have legal make a few changes to the contract we had drawn up to reflect our discussion and get them over to you today. Once you are happy and have signed them, send them back over, and we can get started straight away."

"Perfect. Thank you so much Ms West," he says.

"Oh, none of that," I smile. "If we're going to be working together, please, call me Serena."

The man stands up and extends his hand and smiles.

"Then in that case, I'm John," he replies.

We shake hands and say our goodbyes and the Hislop executives leave the room. I finally relax all the way when I see the beaming smile on Wyatt's face.

"Good job," he says.

"Thank you," I reply, returning his smile. "I hope I didn't overstep the mark with the TV ad stuff, but we hadn't discussed where you sit with it, and I didn't want to lie to him."

"No, not at all. Some people come to us because they want someone to do the designing and what not and they know what they want and that's great. Some people, like Mr Hislop, come to us because we have the expertise and if they do ask you for your advice, then I would always want you to be honest about what would suit them as a company. Even if it means they spend less money, I would rather them be happy and spend less money over a longer period of time than blow their budget and then be annoyed because they got no traction," Wyatt said. "They are more likely to stick with us if they are getting results."

"That's exactly how I would look at it, but some people are just about making as much as they can as quickly as they can regardless of what's best for the client," I say.

"Oh yes, without a doubt," Wyatt says. "But not us. Congratulations on your first client account."

"You mean I get to keep Hislop's?" I ask.

"Of course. That work is all you," Wyatt says. "Now about your party ..."

"Party?" I say before he can go any further.

"Yes, your party to celebrate you landing your first client," Wyatt says.

"Oh, that won't be necessary," I say.

I don't really like being the center of attention at the best of times, let alone here with the boss I've slept with and his personal assistant who is like a bomb waiting to go off and take me down.

"Of course, it will be necessary," Wyatt says, waving his hand as though to wave away my objections. "It's tradition here. When an associate lands their first client, we have a little celebration. I'll have Ruth organize it."

I knew I couldn't argue the point anymore now that he had said that it was something he did for every associate and so I smile.

"Sounds great, thank you," I say.

CHAPTER 21
Serena

I've been down to legal and had the necessary changes made to the contract for the Hislop deal and I've scanned the documents and sent them over. I'm just waiting for them to come back to me. In the meantime, I'm working on the tweaks of where they will be spending their budget, pushing the TV campaign to the back burner and spending more money on targeted social ads and influencer marketing.

I look up when there's a tap on my open office door. I see it's Ruth and although my heart sinks, I smile warmly and invite her in.

"I hear congratulations are in order," she says.

"Ah, I'm just doing my job," I say.

"All the same, it's not often an associate gets their own client this quickly. Well done," she says.

I know how painful that must have been for her and so I smile and thank her.

"Wyatt has asked me to organize your party," Ruth says. "Do you have any dietary requirements? Allergies? Anything like that?"

I shake my head.

"No. Nothing like that. You know, I'm sure you've got enough to do without organizing this as well," I say. "Would you like me to do it?"

"No of course not," Ruth says. "You can't organize your own celebration – that's just too tragic for words. And it's not like it's a huge amount of work. I know Wyatt gets a bit carried away about these things, but it's mostly a couple of glasses of wine and a few canapes in the conference room after work on Friday. Don't get me wrong, it's a nice little ritual, but it doesn't take all that much organizing."

"Ok, no problem, I just thought I would offer," I say.

"Thank you," Ruth says. "It was very kind of you."

She wanders away and I shake my head. That whole conversation had been extremely hard work. I think I prefer it when Ruth is a bitch to me. At least I know where I stand with bitchy Ruth. When she's nice, unless Wyatt is present and it's for his benefit, I always feel like she's planning something or she knows something I don't and it leaves me nervous, which I'm sure she would love.

I am quite surprised that a few of the partners and higher ups in the company come to my office and congratulate me on my first client over the next few hours. I really didn't think it would be seen as that big of a deal. I thought it would be more of a case of if an associate didn't get a client within the first few weeks, they would be history, but it seems that generally speaking, associates just shadow their mentors and do grunt work, at least for the first year or two of their careers. I'm glad I have broken that mold. I had more than enough of doing grunt work when I did my internship.

Another tap on the door gets my attention and I smile as a tall, glamourous looking woman comes in.

"Hi. I'm Beverly, I don't believe we've met. I'm the CFO," she says.

"Oh, hi," I say. "How lovely to meet you. I'm ..."

"Serena, our associate extraordinaire," she finishes for me with a wide smile.

I blush slightly and laugh.

"I don't know about that," I say.

"Well, I do," Beverly says. "And what I say goes."

We both laugh and she sits down on the chair opposite mine. We chat for a while and I really like Beverly, she seems down to earth despite her high ranking within the company and if she wasn't my boss, I could definitely see us being friends. After about ten minutes, Beverly congratulates me again and then she leaves, and I check my email. The signed Hislop contract is in my inbox. I print it out, smiling to myself because now it really is official. I take it and put it in the file with their campaign information. I decide that now I have the contract I can spare five minutes to grab myself a coffee and I head for the break room.

Samantha, another associate, is in there. She turns her head as I enter and smiles at me, and I return her smile.

"Hi," I say. "How's things?"

"Good," she says. "I hear congratulations are in order. Well done, Serena. Seriously. I know how hard landing your first client is."

Samantha is almost two years ahead of me in the associate pathway and she only landed her first client two or three months ago. I don't know what to say. If I agree that it is hard, then it looks like I'm blowing my own trumpet. If I downplay it, it looks like I'm saying Samantha is bad at her job. In the end, I go for the safe answer.

"Thank you," I say, nothing more and nothing less.

It seems to work because Samantha is still smiling.

"Oh, you'll be having your party on Friday, right?" she says, and I nod. "Have you decided what you are wearing yet?"

"I haven't really thought about it," I reply honestly. "Maybe my navy shift dress."

"Navy shift dress? Are you mad?" Samantha says, looking at me in horror as though I am indeed mad and might choose to attack her at any second.

"I ... No," I say.

What's wrong with my navy shift dress? It's business enough for the day's work but it's not like it's horrible or anything. It hits me then what is happening. Ruth is happening again isn't she. She was the one who told me it isn't a proper party. She wanted me to turn up in my work clothes and look stupid. I decide not to tell Samantha that part and just make it look like my own mistake. I don't know if Samantha and Ruth even know each other, let along get on, but I'm not giving Ruth any chance to hear back that she got me and have a good laugh at my expense.

"I'm starting to think I have the wrong idea about this party," I say. "I was under the impression it would be a glass or two of fizz and a sausage roll in the break room after work on Friday."

"Oh God no," Samantha says. "Wyatt will have his assistant book a nice venue and everyone dresses to impress, and we make a full night of it."

"I am so relieved we had this conversation," I say. "God, what would I have looked like being in my work clothes."

"Ah don't worry, disaster averted," Samantha laughs. She gathers her things together and goes and puts her trash in the trash can. "Well, I'd best get back to it. Oh, and for what it's worth, I think your navy dress would have been perfect for the sort of party you were expecting."

"Thanks," I say, glad that at least my dress wasn't that bad.

I now understand her horror though. It isn't even close to appropriate for the sort of event Samantha described, especially not for the guest of honor.

After Samantha leaves the break room, I sit sipping my coffee and thinking. What if for once, Ruth is telling the truth and Samantha just wants to show me up. Maybe it's like an initiation thing. That wouldn't be so bad; if it happened to everyone, I could laugh along with them all. The problem was, if it wasn't an initiation, one of those women wanted me to look ridiculous. And for all I was sure it was Ruth; I didn't know Samantha well and I had to at least consider the fact it could be her. She had been the one to make sure the conversation got onto the party and then my outfit. But that was normal small talk.

Sick of going around in circles, I text Brook. I explain the situation and ask her who she thinks is setting me up. Within seconds, her answer pings back in.

"Ruth," her incoming text message says. Well, that's straight to the point and leaves me no room for doubt about Brook's opinion.

I think that's it, but a moment later and there's another message pinging in from Brook:

"Take a stunning dress to work. Put it on when the working day ends. If Samantha is telling the truth, disaster averted. If it's Ruth (it's not but I know you'll be over thinking again) then you wear the stunning dress, go to the break room, have one drink and say you're sorry, you know this is your party rah, rah, rah, but you have a date, and leave," the second message says.

I smile to myself as I read it. I like that plan and I text Brook back telling her so. She always gives me the best advice. And this particular bit of advice might even have another advantage to it. I mean it probably won't, but it might. It might just make Wyatt jealous to think that I'm out with another man. And even if he isn't jealous, at least he will get to see what he is missing out on and he will know that I'm not sitting around waiting for him to change his mind about me, about us.

CHAPTER 22

Wyatt

I'm on my way back from the bar at the venue Ruth has chosen for Serena's party when the door opens and Serena herself walks in. I know it's not possible and that it sounds like a total cliché, but in the moment when Serena steps into the room, I feel as though time stops still for a minute or two.

I have never seen Serena look so beautiful. She absolutely takes my breath away. She is wearing a long, cream colored dress that looks like it would feel smooth to the touch. Satin maybe. It's a great color that really suits her and it's cut high enough to be classy but low enough to make me want more, and it's backless. The material starts at the top of Serena's ass, and the skirt part flows right to the ground.

Half of her hair is pinned up in a small messy bun and the other half hangs down her back in perfect curls with a few tendrils of curly hair framing her face and stopping the look from being too severe. I don't know if it's her makeup or if she is just happy, but her skin looks radiant, like she is lit up from the inside. God, I want this woman. I want her more than I have ever wanted anyone or anything. I have to have her, but I know I can't have her. I will have to be content just to look at her and drink her in. Fuck I want her. I need her. I have to have her, and I don't think I will be able to stop myself. Why does she have to look that damned good?

She takes a glass of champagne from a passing waiter and thanks him and then she stands and looks around. She looks a little bit lost, like she isn't sure who to go to first. She must feel my eyes on her because she looks in my direction and for a second, our eyes lock and God it doesn't matter what I tell myself, I still want this woman so badly. She smiles and gives me a little wave. I smile back and nod to her. She heads towards me, and I am both eternally grateful that this vision wants to talk to me, and terrified that I can't control myself and I just grab her and kiss her like I want to.

"Wow," I say as she joins me. "You look incredible."

"Thank you," she says, her cheeks flushing. "I was about to say the same about this place. Nice venue choice."

"I wish I could take the credit for it, but it's all Ruth," I say.

"Ah I'll have to remember to thank her," Serena says.

Something in Serena's tone of voice tells me she's not mad about this idea. There is definitely no love lost between the two of them, but I can't for the life of me work out what's wrong there and to be honest, I have decided it's much better for everyone concerned if I keep out of it and just pretend that I don't notice that Ruth and Serena really don't like each other.

Serena and I chat for a bit longer and I introduce her to some of the higher ups in the company as they arrive. She greets them all politely and makes small talk with them, but I think she is relieved when Samantha waves her over. There's a fine line between schmoozing effectively, which I feel like Serena has done, and ass licking, and no one wants to cross that line. Serena waves back at Samantha and then she turns to me with a smile.

"I'll catch up with you later Wyatt," she says. "Thank you again for the party."

She flits away before I can remind her the party is all to Ruth's credit not mine. My eyes follow her automatically as she reaches Samantha, and they kiss each other on one cheek and then the other. I have to force my eyes away. Aside from the fact I'm starting to worry it's creepy if I'm looking at Serena every time she looks up, I'm also worried someone else will notice, and I can really do without that added complication.

Despite myself, I keep looking back at her and as she works the room and chats to the people around her, I can't help but notice that she is still clutching the same glass of champagne she had when she first came in and then came over to me. I like that. It shows she is taking this seriously and wants to be sober when she has to make her speech. I also feel kind of bad for Serena that she's not letting her hair down a bit more. I mean I don't want her to be a drunken mess for her speech, but slightly tipsy is fine and I do want her to enjoy tonight.

I debate going over to her and subtly telling her that she's not at work, she is allowed a good drink. I might even take her a drink over. I stop myself though when I see Serena laughing and joking with the group she's talking to. Maybe she is one of those rare breeds of people who can have a good time at a party without needing to drink alcohol to do so. I admire that.

I'm not one of those people apparently because even as I'm thinking about Serena not drinking, I'm reaching for a glass of champagne. It's not like I'm a raging alcoholic, I just like a drink on social occasions that's all. I spot Ruth coming towards me and I smile and pull her into a hug.

"You sure out did yourself this time," I say, gesturing around the room. "This is awesome."

The venue she has chosen is in a nice hotel. We have the private use of a big ballroom which is all decorated in baby pink and silver, admittedly not the color scheme I would have gone with, but I have to admit that it looks good. There is a disco playing although the dancing most likely won't happen until later. The food is buffet style, and it looks really good. The tables are placed around the edges of the huge dance floor, each one with a crisp white tablecloth and a crisp white cover on the chair, and then alternating between baby pink and silver for the sashes on the chairs and the runners on the tables. It isn't far off being nice enough to be mistaken for a wedding reception.

"Thank you," Ruth says with a smile. "It's a nice place. I think I might use them more often." I nod. "You haven't even gotten to the best part yet. Wait until you try the food. It's absolutely amazing."

"I'm sure it is. I had a little look earlier and I was tempted to peel back the covers and have a nibble," I say with a smile.

"You dare," Ruth laughs, shaking her head. "So, where's the lady of the hour then?"

I pretend to look around, although I know exactly where Serena is. I don't want Ruth to think I'm some weirdo who is watching his staff that closely. She knows me too well as it is and if she thinks I have my eye on Serena like that, she will soon work out that I want to be more than just colleagues with her.

"There," I say, nodding my head in Serena's direction as she nods and laughs at something one of the group of people that she is with is saying.

"Oh, thank God," Ruth says, and I pull my gaze from Serena long enough to frown my question at Ruth. "I forgot to tell her that these parties are the real deal, dress to impress and all of that. It suddenly hit me this evening as I was getting ready to leave that she might think it's just a few pints and a couple of sandwiches, you know? I went to her office to see her, but it was too late; she had already gone. I was worried she would turn up in jeans or come straight here in her work clothes or something."

"Oh, she would have been mortified," I say.

Ruth nods.

"I would have too for not explaining properly to her," she says.

"Oh well," I smile. "Someone obviously told her, so no harm done."

Ruth nods and smiles again. The smile looks fake but why would it be? It's not like her oversight embarrassed Serena and it's not like she had to tell me about her mistake if she didn't want to. She looks at her watch and makes a little oh sound.

"Time for me to start uncovering the food," she says. "Please excuse me."

I nod my understanding and she scurries away. She's probably just uptight until after people have eaten and the food has been a success that's why her smile looked off. I can understand that one. After the food has been served, she will have a drink or two and that's when she'll lighten up. She might even forget herself completely and have a dance.

Serena heads back over to me and I forget about Ruth entirely when she reaches my side and smiles, a nervous looking smile.

"The food will be ready soon," she says. "That means my speech is getting closer."

"Don't worry about that, you'll be fine," I say. "All they want to hear is how much you love them all and how much you love life now that you're one of them."

"Ok, that doesn't sound so bad," Serena says. "Especially considering it's mostly true."

She raises her glass to her lips and takes a long drink of the clear liquid inside.

"A bit of Dutch courage," I joke, looking at glass.

"Oh God no, not before I have to speak in front of everyone," Serena says with a laugh. "It's just tonic water."

"Well make sure you have a few drinks after the speech. This is your night Serena, enjoy it," I say.

"I will," she replies with a smile. "I mean I already am, but you know what I mean."

"I do," I say.

CHAPTER 23

Wyatt

"Ladies and gentlemen," the DJ says over the microphone, momentarily stopping any further conversation between Serena and me. "The buffet is now open."

"I'd best go and find my seat," Serena says, flashing me a smile and disappearing into the crowd once more.

Ruth is right I think to myself as I finish the last of my food. That buffet was amazing, and I definitely think we will be having more events here. I turn to her and tell her as much and she beams.

"I was a little bit nervous booking somewhere new, but I hoped you would like it and our usual place didn't have the right feel about it for Serena. I feel like she wouldn't have felt like enough of an effort had been made," Ruth says.

I resist the urge to role my eyes. I'm not getting into an argument with Ruth here and if I roll my eyes, that's exactly what I know will happen, but I am going to have to address this at some point in the office. It's not a secret to me and probably everyone else in the office knows that Ruth isn't a big Serena fan and that's fine, we don't go to work to make friends, they are just a bonus. But I can't stand the snide little comments Ruth makes about Serena.

It's not even about the fact that I like Serena - it's just not professional to be bitchy like that about an employee or to be seen to condone employees bitching to me about other people. It also annoys me that if Ruth would make the tiniest effort to get to know Serena, she would see that her opinions of her are so far off as to be laughable. Serena obviously will appreciate this place – who wouldn't? – but she would have been so much more comfortable at our usual place, which has more of a chilled-out vibe to it.

"It's time for you to go up and announce Serena's speech," Ruth says after a few more minutes have passed.

I nod and stand up. I take a deep breath as I walk towards the front of the room. The DJ smiles at me and gives me a microphone. I gently pat the top to see if it's switched on. It is and the sound of my touch echoes around the room. I bring the microphone up to my mouth and I start to talk.

"Ladies and gentlemen, if I could have your attention for a moment, please?" I start. I wait for the majority of the chatter to die down and the people to focus their attention on me. I smile again. "Firstly, thank you all for coming. As you all know, this night is a celebration of Serena, our newest associate, landing her first client. I do believe she is the fastest associate ever to get her own client. I have seen the work she has done for that client, and I have to say I am excited for what she is going to bring to the table next. Now before I embarrass her any further, please welcome her up here, Miss Serena West."

I spot Serena standing up. Her dress looks ethereal in the lights and for a moment, her hair shines too, and she looks like an angel. The very sight of her takes my breath away once more and I am glad that I don't have to do anymore of the talking for a moment. I don't think I could keep the quiver out of my voice right now. Serena steps out of the lights and heads towards me and the angelic look fades, but she is still beautiful, even with her cheeks red from embarrassment as she reaches me and feels every eye in the room on her.

I smile and hold the microphone out to her. She takes it and I give her upper arm a quick squeeze to reassure her. I feel the sparks the second my hand touches her skin, and her quiet intake of breath tells me she feels it too. It was probably the wrong move to calm her nerves before her speech, but she can't say I didn't try. I move away and leave Serena in the center of the dance floor.

"Hi everyone," she says, and a cheer goes up. She smiles and I can see the muscles in her back soften slightly. She is relaxing into this. "Don't worry, I'm not going to keep you long. I just want to say thank you to Wyatt for hiring me and for believing in me enough to let me run with my ideas for Hislop's. And I want to thank all of you for the warm welcome. I feel like I have found my home at Smart Marketing Solutions, and I am literally living my dream with all of you. You all rock."

This gets another cheer and Serena pumps her fist into the air. More than half of the room are on their feet now and they fist pump back at her. She turns to me with a much less nervous smile and holds the microphone out to me.

"How did I do?" she says, although I think she already knows the answer to that one.

"Good," I say.

"Ladies and Gentlemen, please give it up one more time for Miss Serena West," I shout into the microphone and the applause keeps coming as more and more people get to their feet. I let it go on for a while, letting Serena have her moment. When it starts to die off naturally, I speak again. "Ok guys, the bar is open, the music is pumping, and the night is young. Let's have fun tonight everyone."

This gets another cheer and another round of applause, and I hand the microphone back to the DJ and go back towards my seat. A few of the staff high five me as I pass. I spot Serena and Ruth at the bar. Ruth hands Serena a glass of something orange in color and hugs her. I raise an eyebrow. I'm shocked to see that, but I can't say I'm not happy about it. I am pleased that Ruth is finally making an effort with Serena, and I'm sure that if she continues to do so she will see the real Serena and start to like her for real.

I realize I should have gone to the bathroom before I came and sat back down and so I stand up and head off to them now. I use the toilet and wash my hands and I come back into the room. A few people stop me on my way back to my table and I find myself laughing and chatting and by the time I get back to my seat, over half an hour has passed since I stood up to go to the bathroom. I scan the room looking for Serena and I can't find her anywhere. I feel a bad feeling in my stomach, but I tell myself not to be silly. She's likely at the ladies' room or something. Or knowing Serena, she's convinced a porter or someone to give her a tour of the place. I smile to myself, but I know she won't really have done that, not in the middle of a work event, although I wouldn't put it past her at a family party.

I still don't see her and when almost ten minutes have passed, I figure she can't possibly still be in the bathroom after all this time unless she is ill. I turn to Ruth.

"Have you seen Serena?" I ask, forcing myself to keep my voice casual.

"She went outside to get some air," Ruth says. She leans closer so only I can hear her. "Not before time if you ask me. She was so drunk she was starting to embarrass herself."

I frown. That doesn't add up at all. At most, Serena has had one glass of champagne and whatever the orange drink Ruth gave her was. Even if that was a double vodka and orange, she wouldn't be that drunk. Even if she'd lied about the tonic water and it had really been vodka too, I still didn't think she'd be drunk enough to be embarrassing herself.

I decide to go and look for her and make sure she's ok, well aware of the possibility that her drink had been spiked, although I hated the idea that anyone who worked for me would do such a thing, I couldn't just ignore it as a possible outcome. I stand up and make my way across the ballroom, not stopping long with anyone who speaks to me, just enough to be polite before excusing myself again. I get out of the ballroom and cross the lobby and go outside. I look to the right. Nothing. I look to the left and see Serena standing there looking at her cell phone.

CHAPTER 24

Wyatt

"Hey," I say, moving closer to her.

"Hi," she replies.

She puts her cell phone in her purse. She doesn't look or sound drunk, but Ruth was at least half right that she's out here, so I'll give her the benefit of the doubt for now.

"Are you ok?" I ask her.

"Yes, I'm great thanks," she says. She smiles. "Thank you for the party."

"Ah, it's no big deal," I say shrugging one shoulder.

"It is to me," Serena says. She looks at me for a moment and then she closes the gap between us, grabs the lapels of my jacket and pulls my face down to hers and kisses me. I'm taken aback but the feel of her lips on mine, with their orangey sweetness, her eager little tongue pushing in between my lips, I can't help but respond to her kiss. I wrap my arms around her, pulling her close, and I kiss her deeply. I never want the kiss to end, but there's a voice in the back of my mind reminding me that she could be drunk, and I could be taking advantage of her, and that anyone from the office could step out here at any moment and catch us. That voice gets through to me and I force my lips away from Serena's and I step back, removing my arms from around her. She lets go of my lapels and frowns at me. She looks hurt and I hate myself for putting that look on her face.

"I'm sorry," I say.

It's lame and it's not enough but it's all I've got.

"If you're sorry for pulling away, then good, so you should be," she says. "But if you mean you're sorry for kissing me, well I'm not sorry it happened, and truthfully I don't think that you are either."

I sigh. I'm not sorry about the kiss. I should be, but I'm not. I am sorry for pulling away though. I could be kissing her now instead of standing here wishing I was. But I won't take advantage of her.

"You're drunk Serena," I say. "I don't want to take advantage of you."

"What are you talking about? I'm not even close to drunk. I've had one glass of champagne and one mimosa," she says.

"But didn't you come out here to get some air because you were drunk?" I say with a frown.

"What? No. I came out because my cell phone rang," she said. "I knew I wouldn't be able to hear inside."

"But Ruth said ..." I start to say and then I stop. "Oh, never mind."

Ruth got it wrong. Serena is as close to sober as if she hadn't even had a drink and she kissed me because she wanted to. I think of the reasons this shouldn't happen even if we are both sober, but suddenly, they don't seem so important and all I want is Serena. I lean in close to her and whisper in her ear.

"To," I say into her right ear and then I kiss her neck.

"Be," I say into her left ear and then I kiss that side of her neck.

Finally, I pull back and cup her cheeks in my hands and look deep in her eyes.

"Continued," I whisper against her lips before I give her a quick kiss there too.

I feel the shiver go through Serena's body and I smile. I'll make her do more than shiver later. I want to kiss her again now, but I am conscious of the fact that anyone could wander out at any moment and it's not a good look for me to be seen ravaging my associate.

"Are you ready to go back in?" I ask.

Serena nods. We walk to the door, and I hold it open for her, and she steps inside. I follow her and we go back to the party. Serena goes off to dance and I go and find Ruth.

"I found Serena," I say.

"Oh good," Ruth says, although her tone of voice says she thinks it's anything but good. "Have you put her in a cab?"

"No, because she's not drunk," I say. "Why would you say she was?"

"She looked like she was stumbling around when she was walking," Ruth says with a shrug. "Maybe she's wearing new shoes."

"Hmm," I say.

"What's that supposed to mean?" Ruth asks.

"Nothing," I say. "I just have to wonder if you're losing your touch at reading people if you can't tell the difference between someone being drunk enough to embarrass themselves or someone having sore feet."

I walk away before she can answer. I'm really not sure what to make of this. I don't know whether to believe Ruth genuinely thought Serena was drunk or not. Ruth is a bit tipsy herself which would affect her judgement, and I know she doesn't like Serena enough to go and check on her herself even if she was falling all over the place.

What worries me more than anything, is how many other people Ruth might have done this to over the years, people I wouldn't have questioned her judgement on. I've always trusted Ruth and her judgment of people and now I have to rethink that. The only reason I've thought twice this time is because of my history with Serena making a lot of what Ruth says not ring true to me.

I'm definitely going to have to keep a much closer eye on Ruth from now on.

CHAPTER 25

Wyatt

I have been dragged onto the dance floor by some of the staff and although I make a protest, I'm secretly quite enjoying myself. The music is pumping, I am a little bit tipsy, and everyone is laughing and having fun, me included. Serena is up here dancing too and it's nice to be able to dance beside her and even with her without it looking suspicious. I just have to be careful to make sure I dance with the others as well, so it doesn't look like I only have eyes for Serena, even though that's the truth of it.

The song ends and the next one starts, and I can't keep the smile from my face when I hear the opening notes of Thriller. It's a good song and I like it, but that's not why I am smiling. It reminds me of Craig and I coming home from college after graduation, and I was hanging out at his place one day when Martin asked him to watch Serena. She would have been around eight years' old at the time, something like that anyway, and Craig and I spent the afternoon teaching her the dance to Thriller.

I don't suppose she remembers after all this time, but

when I look up and catch her eye, she is smiling at me in a way that tells me she does remember it.

A few people have lined up ready to start doing the dance, Serena being one of them. She beckons to me, and I shake my head, but she nods hers and I find myself moving towards her, drawn towards her infectious energy I'm standing beside her doing the moves before I know it.

I lose myself in the music and the movements, movements which come back to me like I danced this dance yesterday not nearly twenty years ago. I'm still very much aware of Serena's presence beside me though and I can't help but throw sideways glances her way, watching the way the fabric of her dress clings to her in all of the right places as she moves. In that moment, I feel such a connection to her that I genuinely don't know how I manage to keep my hands off her, but I do, and I keep waving them and moving.

It's only when the song finishes and the room bursts into applause that I realize everyone else has given up and only Serena and I actually did the full dance. She looks at me, smiling, her eyes shining, and I take her hand in mine, raise it above our heads, and bring our arms down as we bow to the applauding crowd.

Laughing, we go back to our seats, and I have a long drink. I take some teasing from the guys at my table but it's all in good fun and I laugh along with them. I keep thinking of how I felt with Serena moving beside me, how I kept getting little whiffs of her perfume, and how we were so in sync as if we were as good as one.

I can't wait any longer. I don't care about the reasons why we shouldn't do this. I can't fight the way I feel forever. I stand up and announce that I'm leaving. I say my goodbyes and casually tell the table that I'm going to see if Serena wants to share a cab as we only live a few blocks apart.

I hurry away before anyone else asks to share the cab too. I go up to Serena on the dance floor and lean into her ear.

"My place. Now," I say huskily.

She nods, and I can almost smell the hormones coming off her. She wants this as much as I do. She says her goodbyes to a few of the people she is dancing with and then she flits off to find her purse by which point I've called us a cab. I go outside to wait for it, and it pulls up at the same time as Serena appears in the street beside me.

"Good timing," I smile.

She nods and we get into the cab. I can feel the tension in the air, the thrumming of desire that seems to pound not just through me, but through the entire cab. It feels as though the seat beneath me has a pulse of its own, like the roof and the doors have been electrified. I wonder briefly if Serena is feeling this. I don't dare to look at her in case she is feeling the same way and we can't keep our hands to ourselves any longer.

I can't resist touching her though and I move my hand across the middle of the seat until my fingers find hers. She opens up her hand and I slip my fingers between hers and somehow her touch helps. While it drives me wild, it also reassures me that this is real, that Serena really is here and coming home with me, and that she wants this as much as I do.

Finally, after what feels like a lifetime, the cab driver pulls in and tells me the fare. I pay him and get out of the cab. Serena has already gotten out and she stands beside the cab waiting for me. I can see her breath clouding on the air and I can see her breasts moving slightly with each breath she takes. I take her hand and lead her to the front door which I open and let her go in first. I follow her in and close the door behind me. We head for the elevators and go up to my floor. I unlock my front door and follow Serena inside, closing and locking it behind me.

"Would you like a drink? A glass of wine or a coffee or ..." I ask. I stop talking when Serena shakes her head. She takes my hand in hers and leads down the hallway towards my bedroom. I don't have to be shown the way, but I happily follow her. I had been ready to give her another chance to back out, give her another run through of the reasons this is wrong, but with my hand in hers, I can't remember why it is wrong, and it is obvious she wants this. I am really starting to think it can't be wrong if we both want it so badly.

I stay quiet until we reach my bedroom door and Serena almost goes past it. She giggles slightly and back tracks to the right door. She opens it and pulls me into the room, and I kick the door closed behind us. She smiles at me, and I smile back as we stand a foot apart, facing each other. Serena's chest is heaving now, and I know mine is doing the same. It's a mixture of desire and maybe a few nerves now that the moment is finally here. I didn't expect a second chance with Serena and yet here she is, in the flesh, all ready and waiting to be mine.

I reach out and pull her against me and our lips touch. It feels like fireworks exploding on my lips and my skin tingles where she touches me. I run my hands over her bare shoulders as she deepens our kiss, pushing her tongue into my mouth and sucking on mine. I moan as she writhes against me, and I slip my jacket off and then my shirt. I break our kiss long enough to pull my tie off over my head. As I do that, Serena starts on my trousers, opening them and shoving them down, followed closely by my boxer shorts.

I hop on one leg while I untie and remove a shoe and a sock and then I repeat the process on the other leg and then I finally remove my trousers and boxer shorts. I stand naked in front of Serena, and she moans appreciatively as her eyes roam over my body, settling on my cock for more than a second or two, her mouth turning up at the corners in a grin. She looks back up at my face, and her grin is gone. She is serious and full of nothing but lust when she addresses me.

"God, you're fucking hot," she says.

Her voice and her words fill me, and I feel my cock growing harder. I need to get Serena out of that dress and into my bed. I step closer and start to pull the dress down her arms, but she dances back out of my reach and shakes her head. I would be worried she had changed her mind, but she's smiling at me, a teasing little smile, and her eyes are lit up playfully too.

She slips the dress off her arms herself, and it hangs on her hips, leaving her naked from the waist up. I go to touch her breasts and again, she dances away from me. She moves around me in a circle, and I spin, watching her every move. She darts in and foolishly, I think she's coming to touch me and be touched, but no. Instead, she pushes me backwards onto the bed. I go to stand back up and she shakes her head and backs away enough that I can't quite reach her, but I have a good view of her body.

She pushes the dress over her hips and lets it hit the ground. She kicks it away and stays like that for a moment, a vision in white lacy panties. The show is far from over though. She pushes her panties down and kicks them after her dress and then she stands with her feet slightly apart and brings her hands to her chest where she teases herself, kneading her breasts and then playing with her nipples until they harden, and goose bumps chase each other over the surface of her breasts and down her stomach.

God, she's fucking amazing.

She moves one hand away from her breast and runs it down her body and lets it settle between her legs. She moans as she begins to rub her clit from side to side. I can tell by the slurpy sound that she is dripping wet already and knowing that turns me on so much.

She watches me, her eyes locked on mine as she touches herself and it's the hottest thing I have ever seen. Her cheeks are flushed, her pupils are so dilated her eyes look entirely black, and her lips are red and swollen looking. I want to kiss her, taste her, caress her, but I know if I reach for her, she will back away. She is running this show tonight and who am I to stop her when she is so obviously enjoying herself?

Her mouth drops open as she keeps rubbing herself and I know she is close to coming. My cock is going wild; I am so turned on, it is almost painful, and I can't wait any longer. I reach down and wrap my fist around my cock, and I start to move it up and down. Serena sees what I'm doing, and she moans in pleasure as she watches me. The speed of her fingers increases, and her head goes back, and her eyes roll back in their sockets as her hand clenches and her muscles tighten. The tendons in her neck strain as she calls out my name and this time, there is no stopping me.

I go to her and hold her as she climaxes. She lifts her head, and her eyes roll back into place, but she is still touching herself and she is still coming, and she kisses me hard as she moans into my mouth.

Her mouth gets lower, and I stoop slightly to follow it with mine as she kicks her heels off and then she starts to walk with me and this time when she pushes me backwards onto the mattress again, she comes with me. She wastes no time in straddling me and impaling herself on my cock. I feel her delicious warmth, her tight wetness, enveloping me and I sigh in pleasure as I begin to thrust in time with her up and down movements.

I don't care if she still wants to tease me. I can't wait another minute and I need to fill her all the way up before I explode. I need to make her mine. I grab her hips and roll, slamming Serena onto her back and staying on top of her. She wraps her legs around my waist, and we thrust hard.

"You. Are. Mine," I say on each thrust. "Say it."

"I am yours," Serena says, her voice almost a scream as I bring closer to her climax once more. "I am yours."

On the last word, she does scream, and I feel her warm wetness wash over me and that does it. I'm going over the edge with her. I slam all of the way into her, and I come with the tip of my cock pressed against her cervix, her body writhing beneath me. I lean down and kiss her throat as my orgasm floods me and I moan deeply as pleasure assaults every part of me and then, just when I don't think I can take it anymore, it is over as soon as it begun, and I'm left panting and contented.

I slip out of Serena, and I instantly miss her warm folds being wrapped around my cock. I roll off her and get up and lift the duvet up so she can slip into the bed as she gets her breath back. I slip back in beside her and she rolls over to face me. She smiles at me and when I lay down next to her, she leans forward and kisses me.

We hold each other and lay quietly, getting our breath back and enjoying each other's company. I can feel my eye lids growing heavy and I'm almost asleep when Serena speaks up.

"Oh, by the way," she says. "If you say this is a mistake in the morning, I am going to seriously kill you."

She's laughing as she says it, but it makes me realize that last time we had sex and the next day I told her it was a mistake, that I really hurt her. I hate myself for that, but I won't hurt her again.

"The only mistake I made last time was convincing myself us being together was a mistake," I say sleepily.

Serena smiles and runs her lips lightly across mine.

"Correct answer," she says.

I watch her eyes close, and I smile to myself. It was the correct answer because it was the truth. Us being together was likely going to cause some problems with Martin and Craig but they are Serena's family, and they would come around to the idea for her sake and if they didn't, then we would deal with that together. And as for work, well that was the least of my worries. What was I going to do? Fire myself?

I finally fall asleep with a grin on my face at the thought of firing myself.

CHAPTER 26

Serena

I wake up and smile to myself when I remember last night. I'm still in Wyatt's bed, but he isn't here. He can't have gone far – it's his apartment so it's not like he can have gotten up and snuck off in the middle of the night after all. I'm content to just lay here snuggled up all warm and comfortable and wait for him to come back, but my bladder has other ideas and I know I won't be able to get comfortable now.

With a sigh, I get up and look for my clothes. I slip my panties back on and decide the dress is too much for this time of the day. I fold it up and put it on the end of the bed and look around for a robe or something. I don't see one, but I do see a wardrobe and I go to it and open it and pluck out a light blue shirt. I put it on and bring the material to my face, sniffing it, smelling Wyatt's scent on it.

I go off to the bathroom and use the toilet. I find the toothbrush I used the other night is still in the little cup there, so I squeeze some toothpaste out onto it and use it again. I find some mouthwash in the other side of the cabinet and gargle with it and then I wash my face to get the traces of last night's makeup off. I wash my hands and unpin my hair, running my damp hands through it to try and tame the curls down a little bit. I give up after a couple of minutes and I go off looking for Wyatt.

He isn't that hard to find. He's in the kitchen frying bacon. I didn't realize how hungry I am until I smell the bacon and my stomach growls.

"And good morning to you too," Wyatt says with a laugh. "Coffee and juice are already out on the balcony, and the food will be along in a second."

As he's talking, I go to him and wrap my arms around him from behind. When he's finished telling me about the breakfast, he turns around in my arms and kisses me on the lips. I kiss him back and then I go off onto the balcony before he burns the bacon, where I sit down and pour myself a coffee. I add cream and sit sipping it. It tastes like pure heaven in a mug. I am savoring the coffee and admiring the view of the city when I hear the sliding door open, and I look up and admire a different view. Wyatt is wearing a pair of grey sweatpants and nothing else and he looks good enough to eat. I love his six pack and his pecs. I want to run my hands over them, kiss them and caress them.

"What's up?" Wyatt says as he approaches the table and puts down a plate of bacon and waffles. I barely look at them, keeping my eyes on Wyatt's chest. I shake my head, telling him nothing is wrong. "Ok, something is going on. You're being weird."

I force myself to look away from Wyatt's chest and up to his face. I smile.

"I was just admiring the view," I say. "You know it's really not fair that you look that hot in sweatpants."

"It's not fair how much better that shirt looks on you than what it does on me," Wyatt fires back with a smile.

"I was also thinking how much I want to run my hands over your chest," I say quietly. "And then lower, onto your belly. And then lower again."

Wyatt sits down beside me and swallows hard.

"Well, nothing is stopping you," he says.

I grin at him and get up. I move towards him and kneel down on the ground between his legs. I smile up at him and then I put my hands on his pecs. Slowly, I move my hands until his nipples harden, and then I let my hands wander lower and lower, enjoying the washboard feeling of Wyatt's stomach on my palms. Finally, I reach his waist band and he lifts his ass up enough for me to pull his sweatpants down over his hips and ass. I move back long enough to discard the sweatpants and then I move back in towards him.

I take Wyatt's hard cock in my mouth and let my hands roam freely over his chest and belly and his sides. I suck him hard, enjoying the taste of his pre cum and relishing the fact of more to come. I trap Wyatt's cock between my tongue and the roof of my mouth and hum, a trick I learned in a magazine article about driving your man wild.

It seems to work. Wyatt is moaning my name and his hands are now in my hair and tugging on it. It stings my scalp a little bit where he is pulling my hair, but not enough for me to ask him to stop. I keep sucking him, licking up and down his length, making him writhe in his seat. He keeps tugging on my hair, but now it seems more concentrated, like he has a purpose. I realize he's trying to get my attention and I stop sucking long enough to look up at Wyatt, his cock still in my mouth.

He looks down and moans at the sight of his cock in my mouth.

"Fuck it," he says. "I was ready to tell you to stop because I am so close. But I want to come in your mouth Serena. I'll make it up to you after breakfast."

I nod, giving him consent without speaking because to speak would mean to take his cock out of my mouth and I certainly don't want that. I go at him, sucking and licking and blowing. I even lightly nibble on his tip. It's a risky business because he might love it, or he might hate it. He seems to love it. His back arches and his hands grip the chair arms so hard his knuckles go white. He moans my name in a low and desperate voice, and then he lifts his ass off the chair and thrusts once, hard into my mouth, spurting his load into the back of my throat and flooding my mouth.

I swallow and then I suck again, and I keep sucking and swallowing, sucking and swallowing, drinking Wyatt dry. I want to taste him, to drink him in. I suck once more, and Wyatt's only response is a grunted yeah. I think I have drunk him dry, and I release him from my mouth and smile up at Wyatt who smiles himself.

He reaches down and takes my hands in his and helps me to my feet. I start to move back towards my chair, but Wyatt pulls me into his lap instead. He reaches over to the table and pulls the plate of bacon and waffles closer. He picks up a slice of bacon and I do the same. We eat in a comfortable silence and before long, the waffles and bacon are all gone.

Wyatt pours me another mug of coffee and he pours himself a glass of orange juice.

"So," he says as he takes a drink.

"So," I repeat.

"That wasn't a mistake," he says and my heart soars. "Anything that feels that good can't be a mistake, right?"

"Right," I agree. "It was no mistake. So, what does that mean for us then?"

"I ... Before we go any further with this, I need to know if my age bothers you. I am a lot older than you and ..." Wyatt is saying.

"Stop," I say when I've heard enough to know what he's going to say, and he does. "I know it's a cliché Wyatt, but age is just a number. We have something special here and I am not going to risk throwing that away over something as stupid as your age."

"So, we're doing this then?" Wyatt asks.

"We're doing this," I confirm.

We turn to smile at each other, and we kiss. It's a tender kiss, full of passion but also something more, something deeper. As we come apart, I rest my head on Wyatt's shoulder and look out over the city.

"Let's keep it quiet at work a little bit longer," I say. "I still really want to prove myself on my own merit."

That's very much the truth, but I also feel like if it gets out at work that Wyatt and I are seeing each other, everyone is going to have an opinion on us, not all of them good, and I don't feel ready for the whole office to be involved.

"Yes, I agree about work. But we have to tell your dad and Craig sooner rather than later," Wyatt says.

"I know," I say. "But not just yet, ok? Let's just keep it as our special thing for now."

What I don't add because I don't want to ruin the moment is I want to be certain there is more between us than just hot sex before I tell my dad and turn his world upside down. I'm pretty sure that this isn't just about the sex, but it can't hurt to be cautious.

"It will be so much worse if they hear about it from someone else," Wyatt says.

"I know, but no one else knows so we don't have to worry

about that do we?" I say with a smile, and I give Wyatt a quick kiss on the lips. It seems to persuade him.

"Ok, we'll give it a couple of weeks," Wyatt agrees.

CHAPTER 27

Wyatt

I smile to myself as I look back over the copy for Bellisario's new look website. It's good, but that's not why I'm smiling. I'm smiling because when I read it, I can't help but picture Serena when she was putting it together. It started off with a crescendo of her fingers dancing over her keyboard with a pause here and there and then more of the staccato typing. When the typing stopped, then the tongue came out, poking out of the corner of her mouth as she read back through the piece and made some changes. Finally, she showed it to me, and I could feel her eyes on me as I read it and she tried to gauge my reaction to it.

What stuck in my mind about it was the passion with which Serena put together her copy. I could see it in the sparkle in her eyes, the burning red of her cheeks. I loved that she was so passionate about her work, although, as stupid as it sounds, there was a part of me that was a tiny bit jealous, because I wanted to be the one thing she was looking at when she got that expression on her face.

I wouldn't change it though. Her passion doesn't just show on her face when she's working; it shows in her actual work, and it is a part of what sets her so far ahead of the competition. She has skills, but she has passion and drive, and when she's working with a client, that emotion transfers to them and their campaign and she really wants them to smash it. And that is what makes her work so brilliant.

I force my thoughts away from Serena for a moment and reach for my desk phone. I pick up the receiver and call through to Ruth.

"Hello?" she says.

"Hey," I say. "Can you get me Bellisario's on the line please?"

I check the time and do a quick calculation, making sure I'm not calling at a stupid time due to the time zone difference. I work it out to be four thirty in the afternoon in Italy where the company's head office is situated.

"I'm connecting you now," Ruth says.

I thank her and then I hear the click of the call connecting and the buzzing sound of an international call, followed by another quiet click as Ruth hangs up her phone.

"Si?" a male voice says down the line.

"Mr Bellisario?" I ask. "It's Wyatt McAvoy from Smart Marketing Solutions."

"Ah si, si. How are you, Wyatt?" he asks me in English almost as good as mine.

"I'm good thank you. How about you?" I ask.

"I'm good too, and hopefully, I am about to be better. You have the campaign information for me, yes?" he says.

"Yes," I reply. "We have the full rebrand and all of the new branding elements plus a full marketing campaign to roll out with the new brand and generate excitement and drive sales."

"Perfect," Mr Bellisario says. "There is only one problem. I know we initially agreed that I would come to your offices for the briefing and what not, as I was meant to be in America over the next few days, but something has come up and I can't leave the business right now. And I don't want to put off the rebrand. I'm really hoping you can make this work for me."

"Oh, that's not a problem Mr Bellisario. We can do the presentation via a video call," I say.

"No, no," he replies. "This is too important to do on a call. I need to see this stuff in person. I realize it's a big ask, but would you be willing to come to our headquarters in Rome, Wyatt? Your expenses would of course be reimbursed."

I think for a minute. Normally I would say no to such a request. Flying to another continent just to give a presentation with no guarantee of them signing on as a client seemed crazy. But if we got the Bellisario contract, it would push the business up a league and we were already in the big leagues. It would be business suicide to say no because I knew off the top of my head that I could think of at least five other marketing agencies who would be on the next flight if I said no to the request, and while I genuinely didn't believe they were as good as us, they weren't so bad that I could see Mr Bellisario saying no to them all when they had done his bidding and we hadn't.

"Of course, we can come to you. That won't be a problem," I say.

"Great. I have the full morning free on the sixteenth. Is that ok or will it be too soon?" Mr Bellisario says.

I don't want to keep him waiting. If I'm going to go to him, I might as well go tomorrow as any other time. If we fly tomorrow, we can be in Rome for around nine pm local time, just enough time to grab dinner, go over the presentation one last time and get some sleep and be ready for the morning meeting. We can fly back on the evening of the sixteenth.

"Assuming I can get a flight, that's great," I say. "If you don't hear from me, I will see you at ten am on the sixteenth at your offices. If there is a problem with the flights and I can't get there for that date, I will let you know."

"Thank you, Wyatt. See you soon," Mr Bellisario says, and the line goes dead.

Seconds later, Ruth is on the line again.

"Is there anything else you need?" she asks me.

I think for a moment and make a spur of the moment decision, but I feel like it's the right one.

"Yes. Can you find Serena and ask her to come to my office please?" I ask.

"Yes, no problem," Ruth says and then the line goes dead for a second time, and this time, it stays dead.

I don't have long to wait before there's a light tap on my office door and I call out to come in. The door opens and Serena steps in. She says hi and smiles at me, and I smile back at her.

"Ruth said you wanted to see me," she says.

I nod and beckon her in further.

"Yes. Come on in. Close the door," I say.

I watch as Serena closes the door and comes and sits down opposite me.

"So, I have just gotten off the phone with Roberto Bellisario about the rebrand work we have done for him," I start.

"Does he like it?" Serena says.

"I don't know yet," I say. "He was meant to be in the country this week, but he said something came up and he couldn't get away. He doesn't want to do this over a call so I said I would go to him."

"What in Italy?" Serena asks.

"Yes," I say, nodding my head. "And I would like you to join me."

I'm expecting her to be happy about this, maybe even a bit excited, but instead, she frowns, surprising me.

"What is it?" I ask. "I thought you'd be happy at the idea."

"I am," she says quickly. "Only ..."

She stops there and I sigh.

"Only what?" I prompt her.

"Are you asking me to come with you because you want my input in a professional setting or is it just so you have someone to fuck while you're away?" she says.

Well, I didn't see that coming, but I suspect I should have. Serena has always been very vocal about keeping our relationship and our work separate.

"I mean technically, both," I say with a grin. When Serena doesn't return my grin, I turn serious. I stand up and move around to her side of my desk and perch on the edge of it. "What I mean by that is it will be nice to spend some time with you whilst we are there. Or, as you so eloquently put it, to fuck you while we are there." That gets a small grin from Serena and my heart inflates. I love making her smile and laugh. "But this trip is on Mr Bellisario's dime and if you think I'm about to try and explain to him why I needed my girl-friend along on the trip, you are very much mistaken. However, I am more than happy to defend bringing my associate with me who has put as much as I have into this campaign and will be playing an active role in the pitching. Does that answer your question?"

CHAPTER 28

Wyatt

Serena nods slowly and then her face breaks into a wide grin and she jumps to her feet.

"Oh my God, I can't believe I'm going to Italy," she shrieks in excitement, and I can't help but laugh at the sudden turnaround in her demeanor.

"It won't be for long," I warn her. "Assuming the flights are available, we'll leave in the morning and then we'll be flying home the day after."

"I don't care," Serena says, still laughing. "I'm just excited to be going at all."

She jumps up and looks around herself as if she suddenly expects there to be eyes on us. Of course, aren't we're still alone in my office after all. Once Serena is convinced that we're alone, she throws herself into my arms and kisses me. I kiss her back, and I can almost taste her excitement. It's catching; suddenly I find that I too am excited to go to Italy, even if it is just a real flying visit.

Serena's hands move slowly down my back and then around to the front of my body. When she gets to the front of my body, she pulls my shirt out of my pants and then she starts to unbutton my pants. I grab her hands and pull my mouth from hers.

"What are you doing?" I hiss.

"Oh, I'm just showing my boss how grateful I am for a company trip," she says with a mischievous grin and a sparkle in her eye that makes me smile.

"Anyone could walk in," I say.

"Yes," she says. She leans in and kisses me lightly on the lips. "You should really ..."

She stops talking as she starts to squat down, and she kisses my chest through my shirt. She keeps going, her kisses moving lower, and I can feel my cock responding to her teasing touch.

"See about getting a lock for that door," she finishes.

Her mouth is right at my cock height and her hands are working my button again. I realize I have released her hands somewhere along the journey she made down my body. I want nothing more than to let her do her thing, but it's too hard to relax knowing anyone can walk in at any time. I thought that would be a turn on, but it's not when the people walking in on us would be my staff.

As if my thoughts have conjured up my worst nightmare, there is a light tap on my office door at the same time as Serena gets my button open. She looks up at me, that twinkle still in her eye. She kisses my cock through the material of my trousers.

"To be continued," she says, directing the words I used on her at her party back onto me, as I frantically redo my button.

My office door opens without me saying come in, but luckily, I have managed to get my trousers fastened back up and my shirt mostly tucked back in, although I can't help but notice that one of my shirt tails is still hanging out and I'm well aware I look a bit dishevelled because I as sure as hell feel it. Serena on the other hand is back sitting in the chair she had been in before she decided to tease me. She is the picture of innocence as she turns and smiles at the new arrival.

"Hey Ruth, how's it going?" she says, as casually as if Ruth had almost caught her sipping from a cup of tea.

"It's going ok, thank you" Ruth says coldly, an eyebrow raised.

Does she know? Oh, fuck it. If she knows, she knows. I'm not about to ask her what she might have seen, and I think she's far too professional to bring it up with me.

"Ruth, what can I do for you?" I say, recovering some of my wits.

"I have that file you asked for earlier. The Duncan one," Ruth says.

"Oh, thank you," I say, smiling and holding out my hand for it.

I did ask for this file as a priority earlier on today, but I wish Ruth had waited another ten minutes before bringing it to me. Now she's here though, she has more than killed the moment, so I might as well arrange Italy with her to save calling her back again later. Plus, the sooner she tries to get the flights sorted, the better chance we have of getting the ones we want.

"Actually, while you're here, we're going to Rome tomorrow morning and returning the evening after that. Are you free or do you have other plans?" I ask.

"Nothing that I can't cancel," Ruth says.

I nod, glad that she'll be along to keep things running smoothly. I go on.

"I need flights booked and a hotel please. Make sure the hotel is reasonably close to the Bellisario head office as that's where we are going to present their campaign to them in person. Make it a nice hotel. If we land the contract, we can afford to branch out and if we don't, then I will be taking Mr

Bellisario up on his offer to cover the costs of the trip. We will need three seats and three rooms," I say.

Ruth has been entering the information I gave her into her cell phone presumably, so she doesn't forget any of the details of what I need. She looks up from the cell phone.

"Why three?" she asks. "Me and you obviously, and who else?"

"Serena will be joining us. She has worked as hard on this project as I have and she deserves to be in the pitch," I say.

I kick myself internally for explaining myself. I should have just said Serena and left it at that.

"Are you sure that's necessary? The trip will be a whole lot cheaper if it's just the two of us going," Ruth says.

Before I can respond, Serena speaks up.

"She's right you know. About the cost, I mean, not about me not going. Obviously, I'll be going because I'll be a part of the pitch. But there's really no need to drag Ruth along too. I'm sure I can handle taking notes and grabbing a few coffees along with my own job," she says.

She says it so sweetly and so innocently that I know for a fact she was expecting the bristling reaction she gets from Ruth at her words. I have to bite my tongue to not laugh, but at the same time, I value Ruth as a lot more than as just someone who grabs my coffee and I want her on this trip. I decide to intervene before this whole thing gets out of hand.

"While I appreciate you both trying to save the company money, we're not exactly in a place where we need to be watching every last cent ladies. I would very much like both of you to come on the trip. Ruth, if you can arrange that as soon as possible please and let me know the times of the flights," I say.

"Of course," Ruth says.

She glares at Serena for another few seconds before she

leaves the office and closes the door behind her. I'm almost certain she will be standing behind that door for at least a few seconds to see what is being said.

"Ruth is joining us because she keeps everything running smoothly," I say, choosing my words carefully. I want Ruth to hear that I do value her, but I don't want Serena to feel like I'm telling her off. "The fact that you think all she does is make coffee is actually a great compliment to her because it means everything is running so smoothly you don't realize it's because Ruth makes it happen."

Serena shakes her head and waves away my words with one hand.

"I know how much a good PA does," she says, a smile of amusement on her face. "But come on. You have to admit that Ruth takes herself far too seriously sometimes and honestly, it's kind of fun to mess with her."

I have a feeling there's more to it than what Serena is telling me, but if she wanted to say more, she would have, and quite honestly, I have no intention of getting involved in some sort of power struggle between Ruth and Serena. They will figure it out for themselves at some point.

"Right," I say, standing up. "Let 's go and grab some lunch. Are you hungry?"

Serena nods and gets up.

CHAPTER 29

Wyatt

"Won't people talk though if we're seen going out for lunch together?" she says.

"If one of the advertising executives was on the brink of landing a big client and they took their associate out to lunch to discuss the pitch, would you assume they were sleeping together?" I ask.

"No, of course not," Serena says.

"Exactly. And people won't think that about us. It's just because we know we are sleeping together we think others will see it easier. I think Ruth probably has an idea about it though," I say. I look down and see I have tucked my shirt back in at some point while I was talking to Ruth. It's just a reflex action and I don't remember doing it. I look back up. "I was a bit dishevelled when she first came in."

"She's your PA though. She knows better than to gossip about you," Serena says.

"Yes, that's true," I agree. "Come on then. I'm starving."

We leave my office and I stick my head in Ruth's office on the way past.

"I'm going out for lunch. Email me the details of the flights once they are confirmed please," I say.

She nods her acknowledgement and I step back into the hallway and go to the elevator where Serena is waiting for me along with Roland, one of the executives. We greet each other and wait for the elevator. It comes eventually and we get into the elevator. Serena and I stand side by side and Roland stands in front of us.

"The lobby?" he says, his finger poised over the button.

I nod and Serena says, "yes please".

Roland hits the button and then he gets his cell phone out and he starts scrolling through it. Serena reaches out and pinches my ass. I gasp and Roland looks around and I hide the gasp with a yawn.

"Late night last night," I say, ignoring Serena's quiet giggle from beside me.

Roland nods. "I know that feeling," he says, and then he goes back to his cell phone, and I look at Serena with mock seriousness.

"Stop it," I mouth at her with widened eyes.

She smiles and shakes her head and then she runs her hand over my crotch area, teasing my cock. I have to bite back the moan that tries to escape me at her touch. She is looking mighty pleased with herself as she continues to torment me.

"I will get you back," I mouth.

She doesn't respond in words; she just blows me a silent kiss.

By the time we reach the lobby, I'm both glad to be out of the awkward situation of hiding my arousal from Roland, and also gutted to not have Serena be touching me anymore. I am definitely going to get her back for that though. I can't help but laugh though when I address her, shaking my head.

"I can't believe you did that," I say as we cross the lobby.

"What?" she asks, her expression the picture of faked innocence once again. She is getting far too good at this.

"Oh, you know what," I say. I wait until we step into the street, and I look around to make sure no one from the office is around. The coast is clear, and I turn my focus back to Serena. "You should know that you will pay for that little stunt you pulled back there."

"Oh, really?" Serena says with a grin. "I'll look forward to that then."

God, she knows how to turn me on. I want to grab her, slam her against the wall and fuck her against the building right now. I want to devour her. I want to own her. She is mine and she needs to be reminded of that fact as often as possible.

We go to the little deli down the road and get a sandwich each – cheese and ham for me, beef salad for her – and a cold bottle of soda each, and then we sit down at a small table in the back of the place and start working on our sandwiches. We could have gotten the same lunch for free at the office, but we couldn't have spoken freely, and I enjoy our little lunch dates – they break the day up nicely.

"So, I'm guessing you haven't been to Italy before then judging by your reaction to the news you would be going," I say.

Serena shakes her head.

"No. I haven't been anywhere in Europe. A friend and I went backpacking around Asia for six weeks between high school and college. I was kind of tempted to put college off for a year and go and do Europe too, but I talked to my dad about it, and I ended up going to college instead," she says.

"He wouldn't hear of you deferring a year?" I ask.

"Actually, he said he would support me whatever I chose to do, but he pointed out that if I went to college first, I would have my whole life to travel, and if I wanted to do it long term, I would have better job prospects for on the road so I wouldn't have to work eighteen hours a day just to fund my stay," she explains.

"Yeah, that does make sense," I say. "So do you still plan to travel?"

I keep my tone light, but the truth is, I'm suddenly afraid that she will say yes, and then she will get on a plane, and I won't see her for a year. I know it's stupid, but I can't help but think the worst. I'm relieved when she shakes her head.

"Not really. I mean never say never right. But I am more interested in building my career for now. Maybe I'll retire early and travel the world in my fifties," she says with a soft laugh.

"That sounds ideal," I say. "Because by then, you will hopefully have enough money to stay in nice hotels instead of awful hostels."

"Exactly," Serena says. "I'm sorry but these people that say staying in hostels is all part of the experience, have never stayed anywhere nice. I don't think for a second that I can't experience what a country has to offer and still have a nice room to go back to at the end of the day."

That sounds promising. At least if we ever go on holiday together, she's going to let me book a nice hotel and not try to convince me to stay in a hostel or in a mud hut or on a kibbutz or something.

"What about you?" Serena asks. "Did you and my Uncle Craig ever travel?"

"Travel is the wrong word for what me and your Uncle Craig did. We were very much tourists," I say with a laugh. "We'd go to a holiday resort and not even pretend we cared about seeing the sights. It was basically pool, bar, change, night club, repeat."

"So cultured," Serena says with a soft laugh.

"I think I would be more interested in seeing a place now," I say. "And going somewhere that wasn't just a boozy resort. I've been to a fair few different places with the business too but I don't count that."

"Well maybe you don't, but I am very much counting Italy," Serena says.

"Maybe I'll make an exception for Italy," I say.

Serena nods.

"You'd better. It's our first trip away together," she says. "One of the most romantic cities in the world and we'll be there. Me, you, and fucking Ruth."

I burst into laughter at the change in her tone when she reminds me that Ruth will be on the trip with us.

"She won't be with us all of the time," I say.

"I hope not," Serena says. She smiles then, and that mischievous look from earlier comes back over her face. "But just in case we can't shake her, I had better get some practice in."

I open my mouth to ask her what she means when I feel her foot on my leg.

CHAPTER 30
Wyatt

She walks her toes up my shin and over my knee and then she rubs it against my inner thigh. My cock responds to her touch like it always does, coming to life instantly, but I force myself to think of things other than Serena and how fucking good her touch feels, and I keep it down.

"Stop it," I say quietly.

"Why? Don't you like it?" Serena says as she moves her foot higher.

"You know full well I like it. Now knock it off," I say.

Even as I say it, I'm spreading my legs to give her foot access to where it wants to be. She presses the sole of it against my cock and then she rubs it over me. I'm really struggling to not get a hard on. I'm really struggling not to grab Serena and kiss her teasing little mouth as well.

I finish the last bit of my sandwich and look Serena in the eye as I drink the last of my soda. I can see the desire in her eyes, and I know that for all this is fucking torture for me, it's affecting her too. Somehow, that makes me feel better. I keep watching her as she finishes her lunch and teases me. I feel my hands balling into fists on the table as the sensation becomes so intense that I'm sure I'm not going to be able to control myself anymore. But I manage it. Somehow, I manage it.

I know it's not going to last forever though and as much as I'm enjoying this playful side to Serena, I'm not going to risk embarrassing myself in public that way and so I take a deep breath and stand up, leaving Serena's foot behind.

"Are you ready to head back?" I ask.

She nods and wrinkles her nose at me and calls me a spoil sport, and I know she knows why I've called an end to the lunch. I offer her my hand and help her up from her seat and then I go to the counter to pay while Serena goes to use the bathroom. We meet back up out at the front of the deli and head back towards the office.

"I suppose, seeing as this was meant to be a working lunch, I should at least ask you. Is there anything in the pitch you are not happy with or are unsure about?" I ask.

Serena shakes her head and smiles.

"I have been over it so many times I think I could probably recite it without the slides," she says.

"I know that feeling," I say, laughing with her.

We arrive back at the building and cross the lobby. We wait for the elevator, and I decide it's time I paid Serena back for her teasing little touches. We are the only ones waiting and when the elevator arrives, I gesture for Serena to get in first. I follow her in and press the button for our floor and then I stay next to the control panel.

It seems to take forever for the doors to start to close and the whole time, I'm thinking to myself come on, close. Close for fuck's sake. After what feels like an eternity, the doors finally start to close. Of course, at that exact moment, a woman starts to run towards the elevator.

"Hold the elevator please," she calls.

When my hand doesn't move, Serena frowns at me and reaches around me to press the button to hold the doors. I know that's the right thing to do, but I'm so past that and so ready for taking Serena that I don't care anymore. I knock her hand away.

"Sorry, this one's taken," I say as I press the button for our floor again.

The doors close and the elevator starts moving. I can imagine how annoyed the woman is and I don't care at all.

"What the fuck was that?" Serena says. "Why didn't you hold the elevator for that woman?"

"Because if I had, I couldn't have done this," I tell her as I pull the emergency stop lever.

The elevator screeches to a halt and Serena's confusion turns to a smile as she works out what's happening.

"It's time to find out what happens when you tease me all day," I say to her.

Without another word, I pull her to me and lift her dress up past her hips. I push her panties to one side as she gets fully with the program and fumbles my pants open. In a series of breathless kisses and fumbling, I am inside of Serena and she's as tight and as wet as ever. I love how wet she is. It lets me know that I was right - she was teasing herself as much as she was teasing me back there in the deli.

I pull out of Serena long enough to turn her around. She turns willingly and bends over for me, her legs spread with her palms on the wall supporting her. I slam back into her, and she moans as I fill her all the way up. I don't waste any time. I'm already on the verge of coming and judging by how wet Serena is, I'm not the only one. Plus, I know if I take too long, maintenance will be down to see what's happened to the elevator.

I slam in and out of Serena, holding her hips and moving her with me. She cries out as I fill her up, and I move one hand from her hip and move it to the front of her body. I have barely touched her clit when she comes. She was already so close that it didn't take more than a brush over her sensitive parts. She comes hard and she bites down on her hand to keep her scream inside.

I feel her flood of warm juices and I can't hold back anymore myself. I come with Serena, whispering her name as I hold onto her hips again, keeping myself deep inside of her as pleasure assaults my body. I give another thrust, pushing in even further and Serena shudders and her pussy tightens around my cock, and I moan her name as my climax takes me away from reality for a moment.

I come back to myself and slip out of Serena, already missing the feeling of her delicious heat around my cock. She straightens up and puts her panties right and pulls her dress down as I tuck my shirt back in and fasten my trousers. Our chests heave as we make ourselves presentable once more. I reach out and cup Serena's chin in my hand and use my thumb to wipe off the smudge of lipstick from her chin. It feels like a strangely intimate gesture and when I've wiped the lipstick away, I gently kiss her lips. She smiles and looks into my eyes as I step back from her.

I reach behind me and press the emergency stop button back into place and the elevator starts to move again. Wordlessly, Serena and I look at each other and together, we both start to laugh.

"So, you know how that was meant to be you getting your own back on me for teasing you?" Serena says through her laughter, and I nod. "Well, I hope you don't think that's going to stop me. If anything, it has just ensured I will do it all the more."

"I hope that's a promise and not just an empty threat," I say and then the doors to the elevator ping open on our floor and we have to go back to being professional. I want to push her back into that lift and stay locked away in there with her all day, but I know we can't do that and with a sigh, I go back to my office and Serena goes back to hers.

Once I'm back in my office, I check my emails and find one from Ruth with our flight details. I'm pleased she has managed to get the flights at such short notice, and I reply thanking her and then I forward the email to Serena with a message telling her what time I will be picking her up to go to the airport.

CHAPTER 31

Serena

I'm in heaven as we get out of the taxi. Or at least the nearest thing to it. I spin around and take in the beautiful piazza, and the huge, amazing fountain. A huge stone sculpture forms the backdrop to the fountain, giant figures overlooking the water and the tourists beneath them, many of whom face away from the water and toss a coin into the fountain over their shoulder.

"Why are they doing that?" I say to no one in particular, but the taxi driver, who is busy getting our luggage out of the trunk of the taxi, hears me and replies.

"That's the Trevi Fountain," he says. "Legend has it if you throw a coin in over your shoulder like that, one day, you will return to Rome."

"Oh," I say. "I'll have to make sure to do it. I have only been here five minutes and I am already in love with the place."

"It's a beautiful city," the taxi driver agrees.

He gets the rest of our luggage out of the trunk as I watch the small crowds of people passing by. No one seems hurried. People stroll along taking in the sights and the sounds and the smells and I love that it's such a different pace of life here.

Finally, our bags are all out of the trunk and the taxi driver has been paid. Ruth points to a beautiful building right on the fountain.

"That's us," she says, and I have to admit she has chosen our hotel well.

I grab my case and my laptop bag and follow behind Ruth and Wyatt as they head for the hotel. We reach it and step inside, and the air conditioning does its job, the cool air rushing over my hot skin. It feels amazing and I take a second to just enjoy it and then I look around. The floor is tiled in a warm gold color and the fixtures and fittings match, the reception desk and the walls matching the gold color and the chairs and tables spread throughout the lobby have gold frames and red cushions. The whole place is bathed in a warm yellow light, and it should be as gaudy as all hell, but it isn't. It is regal looking and yet comforting, like coming home.

Ruth leads us to a cluster of the seats.

"I'll go get us checked in," she says. "Can someone watch my stuff?"

I nod and Ruth goes to join the short line at the reception desk. Wyatt and I sit down around a low coffee table.

"This place is gorgeous. Have you stayed here before?" I ask Wyatt who shakes his head.

"No, but you're right, it's really nice and it's in a good location too," he says. "The client's offices are just down the road, and we definitely can't complain at the view."

"No, it's beautiful," I say. "Even if we're at the back there's a lovely little square there, just no fountain."

I spotted it on the way in and noted that it looked like a fun place to visit. Not that I'm here to visit anywhere but Bellisario's, but I can dream.

Ruth appears back at our sides holding three key cards.

"All done," she says, sitting down on one of the empty seats. "Two of us are on eight and the other one is on seven, but we all have views of the fountain. The two on eight are adjoining rooms, which I didn't know when I booked. I explained we're work colleagues not a family and the response from the receptionist was to tell me to lock the connecting door. So should you and I take those rooms Wyatt as we know each other the best?"

I really want to have an adjoining room with Wyatt. It'll be perfect for us to sneak in and out of each other's rooms without risking Ruth catching us, but I can't think of any argument to Ruth's point. Luckily for me, Wyatt can and does come up with something.

"No, actually, I think it makes more sense for Serena and me to take the adjoining rooms. It'll save us trekking from floor to floor to go over the pitch and make any changes," Wyatt says.

Ruth does not look happy about that, and she is shaking her head.

"Daniel, it might make Serena uncomfortable," she says. "It will be like you are practically sharing a room."

"Serena, do you trust me to not attack you in the night?" Wyatt asks.

I nod, not trusting myself to speak in case I laugh. Ruth rolls her eyes.

"Well, she's not going to admit it if she doesn't, is she?" she says.

"Look Ruth, the discussion is over. I've made the decision. Serena and I will take the rooms on the eighth floor, and you will take the room on the seventh floor. Hand over the keys please," Wyatt says firmly, and I feel my clit pulse. I love it when he gets all alpha like that.

His cell phone buzzes, and he takes it out of his pocket with one hand. His other hand is stretched out to Ruth to get the room keys. I'm looking anywhere but at Ruth and trying my best not to smirk as Ruth finally gives up the key cards. Wyatt looks down at his cell phone once he has them and Ruth turns to me, and I can't look away quickly enough to not catch her eye. The icy cold stare she gives me makes me feel as though I should literally just shrivel up and die.

I don't bite. I don't roll my eyes, although I want to. I don't ask her what's wrong. I just continue as though she isn't there. The truth is, I know she's only jealous and honestly, who can blame her? I'd be jealous if someone else had Wyatt and I would probably be throwing eye daggers at them too.

Wyatt finishes whatever he was doing on his cell phone and puts it away. He looks up at us and Ruth instantly puts her face straight. Wyatt checks the time.

"OK, it's almost six o'clock. What do you both say we go to our rooms and unpack and freshen up and meet back down here at seven thirty to go and have dinner?" he says.

I nod. That works for me. I'm looking forward to a nice shower more than anything.

"Yes, that's fine," Ruth says with a smile that actually doesn't look fake. I resist the urge to roll my eyes again – something that is becoming quite common for me when I'm around Ruth - as we stand up and gather our things and head for the elevator.

We get in with a few other people. Some get out as the elevator climbs, but even once Ruth gets out on the seventh floor reminding us of the meeting time, there are still other people in it besides us. A glance at the control panel tells me there are at least two more floors above us. I say at least because sometimes the really good suites aren't on the panel as they have their own elevator.

The elevator pings again and the doors open, and it is mine and Wyatt's turn to leave the elevator. We step out onto a tiled floor that matches the one in the lobby and we follow the arrows until we come to our rooms. Wyatt gives me one of the key cards and keeps the other one for himself.

I smile at us standing side by side at our doors ready to go in. I don't know why the image strikes me as funny, but it does. Wyatt looks at me questioningly and I just shake my head. He wouldn't get it. No normal person would.

"See you at seven thirty," I say, and he nods his agreement and I open my door and go into my room.

CHAPTER 32

Serena

I t's a lot hotter in the room than it is in the public areas of the hotel, but I soon see why. It's one of those systems where you have to put a key card in the slot to work the lights and the air conditioner unit. I put my key card into the waiting slot and smile as the little light goes green and then I hear the air conditioner unit rattle into life, and I instantly feel cool air coming in towards me.

I look around the room. It's a nice size, easily big enough for the two people it's aimed at judging by the double bed. The bedding is white with a red runner, all of which looks clean. The theme of gold and red has continued up to the room and again, it isn't too much, it's perfect.

Other than the double bed, there is a dressing table with a stool which can easily double up as my work desk. There is a wardrobe, with a set of drawers in the bottom and a bedside cabinet on either side of the bed. A glass sliding door opens out onto a large balcony and beside the balcony doors is a red plush chair. There is also a fridge and a tea and coffee making area on a tiny table next to the dressing table.

I slide the door open and slip out onto the balcony. There are two sun loungers and a small table between them. I walk past the loungers to the balcony wall, and I look out over the square. We got the fountain view alright – thank you Ruth - and it's every bit as magnificent as I thought it would be. I have to bite my lip to stop myself from making a squeal sound with excitement.

I go back into my room, and I decide to go and check out the bathroom. There are two doors, one slightly ajar, which is the bathroom door. The other one is closed, and it has a bolt pulled across it and I feel butterflies in my tummy when I realize that's the adjoining room door. Wyatt is just on the other side of it. I debate opening it and slipping into his room, but I really do need to shower and change and if Wyatt and I get together, it likely won't happen.

I go into the bathroom instead, as I originally had planned to do. Again, it's a good size and it has a bath with an over bath shower, a sink and a toilet and a bidet. There are a few small toiletries laid around, but I've brought my own shampoo and what not, so I don't really take a lot of notice of those.

I go back into the main room and start to unpack. I haven't brought a lot because I knew how short of a time we would have here. I hang up my clothes and look at my sad little wardrobe with two outfits in it; one smart but casual for tonight and one work based one for tomorrow. I will change back into the leggings and tunic top I'm currently wearing to fly home in.

I unpack the rest of my things – my toiletries, my makeup, that kind of thing, and after a few minutes, I'm done. I take my laptop out of its carry bag and place it on the desk. I put the bag inside of my suitcase and then I stow my suitcase in the bottom of the wardrobe and then I strip off and head for the bathroom. I have a lovely cool shower and come back to the room. I put my makeup on and get dressed. I need to dry my hair, but the thought of blasting my head with heat isn't exactly an idea I like so instead, I go back out onto the balcony and let the sun dry it. I still have an hour until I have to meet the others; that'll be more than enough time for my hair to dry.

At around seven fifteen, I hear a knock on my door. I get up and go into the room.

"Two seconds," I call.

I quickly run my brush through my almost dry hair and spritz myself with perfume. I go to open the door. I'm expecting Wyatt or Ruth, but nobody is there.

"What the hell?" I ask.

I look up and down the hallway for any signs of life but there's no one in sight in either direction. I close the door, confused and a little bit annoyed at being disturbed for nothing, but it's almost time to go anyway so I guess I can't moan that much. I slip my feet into a pair of white wedges that match the white three-quarter length trousers I'm wearing with a soft pink vest top. I grab my purse and check that I have my cell phone and my debit card, both of which I do. I just need my key card on the way out.

As I'm thinking about not forgetting the key card, the knock comes again and this time, a voice calls out with it.

"Serena? I know you said hold on, but come on," the voice says.

It's Wyatt's voice and as I hurry to open the adjoining door, I'm laughing. I get it open, and Wyatt looks at me.

"What's funny?" he asks.

I tell him how I went to the main room door and how I got a little bit miffed that I had been disturbed by someone who couldn't even hang around to tell me what they wanted and then realized I had answered the wrong door. He laughs and shakes his head.

He pulls me into his arms and kisses me gently on the lips and then he holds me out at arm's length.

"You look great," he says.

I know he's only being nice – my outfit is nothing special – but it's still nice to have him compliment me and I smile and thank him.

"Are you about ready to leave? I can't handle the headache I'll get off Ruth if we're late," Wyatt says.

I know he means if he is late. Ruth would love it if I was late, and she got some alone time with Wyatt. Well sorry bitch, that's not happening anytime soon.

I nod and smile.

"Yeah, let's go," I say. "See you in the corridor in two."

Wyatt nods and I go to pull the door closed but he shakes his head. I frown and he smiles.

"I want to watch your ass as you walk away," he says.

I throw my head back and laugh but he's serious and I think fuck it and I turn and walk away, letting him watch the show. I even put a little sway into my walk so my hips go from side to side more than they usually would. I hear Wyatt whistle softly from behind me.

"That's what I'm talking about," he says and then the adjoining door shuts. I can't help but smile even as I shake my head in amusement.

I grab my purse and get my key card out of the slot and put it in my purse and then I step out of the room and see Wyatt doing the same thing next door.

"Well fancy meeting you here," I say with a laugh.

"Yes, such a strange coincidence," Wyatt agrees.

He offers me his arm and I take it and for a few moments, until we reach the elevator, it's like there's only me and him in the whole world. Of course, that isn't true though. Hell, it isn't even only me and him for dinner. It's a nice thought while it lasts though.

CHAPTER 33

Serena

"Oh my God, that was amazing," I say as I swallow the last bite of my pizza. "It has officially ruined the rubbish we call pizza back at home for me forever though."

"Ah American pizza isn't so bad. It's just totally different to what the Italians call a pizza," Wyatt says.

"You're not kidding," I reply. "Did you enjoy yours Ruth?"

To say dinner has been awkward would be the understatement of the year. Ruth has barely said a word unless Wyatt or I have asked her a direct question and that became so awkward, Wyatt and I mostly stopped talking too just passing the occasional comment about the food. I decide to have one last try to bring her into the conversation now that she's had two glasses of wine.

"Yes, thank you," she says.

Well, that worked then.

"Did it ruin home pizzas for you?" I press her.

She's quiet for so long I don't think she's going to bother answering me, but then she finally speaks.

"I think it's like Wyatt said. If you think of them both as the same thing and compare them, the Italian one will always win hands down. But if you think of them as two separate things, then I see no reason why we can't enjoy both," she says.

It's not really an answer to what I asked her, but it's the most she's said all night, so I'll take it.

"Anyone for dessert?" Wyatt asks.

"Not for me thank you," Ruth says instantly.

If I thought she would leave and Wyatt and I could enjoy dessert together, I would say yes, but as much as I'm not a big Ruth fan, I'm not about to let her wander off on her own at night in a foreign country and I'm sure Wyatt wouldn't either. I shake my head, praying Wyatt doesn't want one either and we can end this awkward meal once and for all.

I'm relieved when Wyatt catches the waiter's eye and makes the signal for the bill. I don't actually think Ruth has made this dinner awkward on purpose, because she looks as relieved as I feel when she sees Wyatt requesting the bill. I think it's just a case of me and her not really getting along and no one knowing which topics of conversation would be safe ground and which ones wouldn't be. And I think for Wyatt, it must be just as awkward being stuck in the middle and if he sits and chats and laughs with me, he feels like he's leaving Ruth out and if he sits and chats and laughs with Ruth, he feels like he's leaving me out.

The waiter comes with the bill which Wyatt pays and then we leave. We head back to the hotel without it being a discussion. We step inside the lobby. There is a bar area off the lobby that looks pretty lively and for a moment, Ruth looks into it, and I speak up before I really think it through.

"Do you want to grab a night cap, Ruth?" I ask.

For a moment, I think she's going to say yes, and I don't know if that's a good thing because we can let this silly

179

awkwardness go or whether it's a bad thing because we won't be able to just let it go like that. I'm saved from ever finding out which it would have been though.

"I think I'm just going to call it a night. It's been a long day and we have an early start tomorrow. Thank you for the invite though. Another time maybe," she says, and I smile and nod.

"You're probably right. I think an early night is probably the best idea," I say.

We all go to the elevator and ride up. When it reaches the seventh floor and Ruth says goodnight and gets out, it feels like the air lightens and when the doors close again, Wyatt and I both breathe a sigh of relief.

"Please tell me I'm not the only one who thought that whole dinner was as awkward as hell," I say looking up at him.

He shakes his head.

"No, it wasn't just you. What on earth were you thinking asking if she wanted to go for a drink with you?" he says.

I shrug my shoulders.

"I don't know. I felt a bit sorry for her. She was always your golden girl and now she's got competition and she's losing, and I feel bad for her," I say.

Wyatt raises an eyebrow as we get out of the elevator.

"She's losing, is she?" he says.

"Oh, yeah. By a country mile," I say.

We are at our room doors and Wyatt smiles at me.

"Your place or mine," he says.

"Actually, I really want to go over the slides one more time," I say. "So how about you give me like an hour, and I'll knock on your door when I'm done."

"Ok," Wyatt says. I know he wants to argue the point, but I also know that he won't because he wants this pitch to go as well as I want it to go. He leans in and kisses my cheek. "Don't be too long or I might fall asleep waiting for you."

"I'm sure you can find something to do to keep yourself awake," I say. "Now if you'll excuse me, duty calls."

I open my purse and get my key card out and open my door. I smile at Wyatt, and he smiles back and then I step into my room and let the door close behind me. I put my key card in the slot and wait a second for the lights to come on. Once they do, I put my purse on the bed and kick my shoes off and then I open the fridge and pull out a bottle of water. I open the water and have a long drink and then I open up my laptop and switch it on. I sip my water while I wait for it to boot up, but nothing happens.

The battery must be low. I tut to myself and go to the wardrobe. I get my suitcase out and then the laptop bag so that I can get the adaptor out. I put the bags back away and go back to my laptop. I connect the adaptor and then I plug it in, and the green bar appears on the screen telling me it is charging but that there isn't enough power to use it yet. I take another drink while I wait, but it soon becomes obvious to me that this is going to take forever, and I want my laptop fully charged before tomorrow. I am awfully glad I decided to have one last look at the pitch, or I wouldn't have known it wasn't charged. I was so sure that the battery was full. Oh well. I sigh and get up and go to the adjoining door to tell Wyatt I'm going to be stuck having a late one and he may as well go to bed.

I tap on the door and open it. I half expect Wyatt to be asleep already, but he's sitting up on the bed with his own laptop open on his knee. He has changed out of the shirt and jeans he wore for dinner and now he's only wearing a pair of navy-blue colored shorts. He looks so hot. God, I want him so badly. But no. Work first, play later.

"That was quick," Wyatt says, looking up from his screen.

"My computer battery was dead. It's going to take a while I think and then I still want to run through the pitch, so you may as well go to bed when you're ready," I say.

"Oh no. Nuh uh. No way," Wyatt says, putting his laptop down on the bed beside him. I frown at him. "There's no way you're ditching me on the one night we're spending in the most romantic city on earth. We can go through it together on my laptop."

I like that idea. I really want to spend the night with him too. I smile and nod and step fully into his room.

"That sounds like one of your better ideas," I say.

I walk towards the bed, but Wyatt gets up.

"Wait, before we start, there's something I want to show you," he says.

"What?" I ask.

He holds his hand out to me, and I take it and he leads me towards the sliding door to the balcony.

"You need to see this beautiful view," he says.

"Oh. I've seen it. It's the same from my room. It really is spectacular, but ..." I say.

I don't finish because Wyatt is softly shushing me, and I wonder what is going on. Is there something out there that he's hiding from me? Oh my God, is he going to propose? No that's ridiculous. We've only been dating for five minutes. I think I would say yes though if he did. Hell, I know I would.

CHAPTER 34

Serena

Wyatt opens the door and pulls me through it and there's nothing there. No candles. No champagne. No ring box. Obviously. He leads me to the wall and then he stands beside me. He points down at the now lit up fountain.

"How beautiful is that?" he says.

The view takes my breath away and now I'm glad I didn't put up too much of a fight about coming out here. I hadn't realized how much more beautiful the city would look in the dark.

"It's gorgeous," I say, my voice quiet and awed.

"And how about this?" he says.

He moves behind me and before I know it, he's pushed his hand between my legs, and I'm kind of straddling his arm. He rubs my clit through my clothes, and I bite my lip to stop myself from moaning.

"What are you doing?" I say, in a half whisper.

"This," Wyatt replies, still rubbing me.

I'm getting more and more flustered as he applies more

pressure on my clit, but I'm still aware of where we are. I grab his wrist and pull his hand away.

"Stop it," I say. "Anyone could see."

He gently takes my hand off his wrist and moves his hand back to my clit.

"Shh. No one can see," he says. "Look. The wall of the balcony is solid. Anyone on their balcony or looking out of their window will just see you standing there looking out at the city."

He moves his hand away himself this time and gets one of the loungers. He pulls it closer to me and perches on the end of it.

"See? No one will see me. So, assuming you can control yourself and not scream when you come, we're good," he says with a wicked looking grin.

"I'll try," I say, and it sounds sarcastic, but I don't mean it that way. I genuinely do mean I will do my best to be quiet, but I can't guarantee it.

Wyatt grabs my waistband and pulls my trousers down. I step out of them and then he follows them with my panties, and again, I step out of them. I turn back to face the city and Daniel's expert fingers go to work on me.

At first, staying quiet isn't so hard. Wyatt is waking my clit up and my pussy is coming to life, but it's nothing I can't handle. I mean don't get me wrong, it's nice, but it's not quite at the 'scream his name on a wave of pleasure' level of nice yet. He moves my clit gently from side to side and I move with him, trying to get him to press harder. His touch is merely teasing me right now.

He takes the hint, but then he does something he's never done to me before. His hand is coming in from the direction of my ass and he sticks his thumb into my pussy and then he keeps moving his index and middle fingers forward through my lips. They end up on either side of my clit and Wyatt gently presses his fingers together, sending shockwaves through my sensitive clit. At the same time, he rubs the inside of my walls with his thumb and finds my g spot.

He continues to work on my clit as he also works my g spot and now staying quiet is getting harder. I'm fizzing, desperate for an orgasm but also not wanting this to end. It's intense, maybe even a little strange but my God it's good. I rock my hips, forcing more pressure onto my clit and Wyatt obliges, squeezing and rubbing it harder and pressing harder on my g spot. My stomach rolls deliciously and then for a moment, I feel like I might pee. The moment passes and I'm floating on pleasure, only Wyatt's hand on me stopping me from floating away.

I'm hurtling towards my orgasm and despite where I am, I know this isn't going to be quiet. I also know I can't ask Wyatt to stop now. I think I would explode with frustration if he did. I think fast and cross my arms on the balcony wall in front of me. I press my mouth against my arms and as I hit my orgasm, I let out a cry that my arms muffle enough to make it not too obvious it's a sex noise.

Fireworks spread through my body, my nerve endings sizzling and firing off. My clit is pulsing hot waves of pure pleasure through me, and my pussy has clenched tightly around Daniel's thumb which is still working my g spot. My nipples are so hard and the skin on my whole body is covered in goose bumps as the pleasure sends shivers through me.

I cry out into my arms again when Wyatt pulls his thumb out of me and puts his mouth on the edge of my pussy. He licks and sucks, lapping up my juices and devouring them, devouring me with them.

By the time he finishes, and I have climaxed again, my arms on the wall aren't just keeping me quiet. They are also keeping me from collapsing into a heap on the ground. I hear Wyatt stand up beside me and then I feel his hand on my lower back and his lips on my neck and I force my head up from my arms.

"Wow," I say. "Thirteen out of ten."

"And you get like a seven out of ten for staying quiet," he says with a laugh and then he kisses me, and I go to wrap my arms around him, but I forget about my numb legs, and I'm falling.

Wyatt catches me without missing a beat and he scoops me up in his arms and carries me back inside of the room and to his bed. He leaves the balcony door open and the breeze that washes in is nice on my hot skin.

Wyatt lays me on the bed and kicks his shorts off. I take the opportunity to pull my vest top off and ditch it over the side of the bed. Wyatt looks down at my now naked chest and grins and licks his lips, and then gets on top of me and now I do wrap my arms around him and he's inside me, thrusting and moaning as he fills me up. I grab his ass cheeks, pushing him deeper and deeper into me until it feels like we are one. We move as one, we cry out as one, and we orgasm as one. We are one.

Pleasure floods me once more and this time, I'm not alone. Wyatt is coming too, and I can feel his body going rigid as his cock spurts and twitches inside of me. I tighten my pussy and he moans my name in a voice that is all sex and a shiver goes through me, followed by another climax as Wyatt's pubic bone hits my clit as he thrusts into me again mid orgasm.

I dig my nails into his ass cheeks as my hands curl up into balls and my whole body sort of pauses, like I'm just hanging there, suspended in space and time and all I can feel is my clit and the pulses of sheer ecstasy that it is pushing out around my body.

I can't breathe. I can't see. But it doesn't matter. I can feel and that's all I need to be able to do in the moment. I can feel Wyatt inside of me, his own orgasm finishing. I can feel my clit still working its magic and I can feel Wyatt's lips on mine.

I float back down into myself, and I can see again, and I can breathe again, and I'm panting for breath like I've been starved of oxygen for a week rather than the twenty or so seconds it actually must have been. I'm still getting pulses through my pussy that make my muscles there spasm uncontrollably and each time it happens, a delicious little spark goes off in my lower belly.

Wyatt pulls out of me and rolls to the side, narrowly avoiding sending his laptop crashing to the ground. Judging by the faraway look on his face, I don't think he would have noticed if he had knocked it down. We lay side by side, our heads turned to face each other as we slowly come down.

I look deep into Wyatt's eyes and as much as I want this to go slowly and for us to be sure this is what we want, all I can see is my future reflected back at me. I realize in that moment that I never want to not be able to lose myself in those eyes. I smile and I'm about to tell Wyatt what I'm thinking when I realize that I can no longer see his eyes because they are closed.

His breathing deepens and I watch his chest rise and fall for a moment. I feel bad for needing to wake him up. It's been a long day and I know how tired he is because I'm the same, but I know I won't sleep until we have looked over the pitch one more time.

"Wyatt." I whisper. He doesn't stir. "Wyatt?"

I say it louder the second time and he makes a 'mmm' sound but he doesn't open his eyes.

"Wyatt, wake up," I say, shaking him gently.

"I'm awake," he says but still his eyes are closed and before I can even speak, his breathing has evened back out.

I decide to try one more time and if he still doesn't wake

up, I will go back to my own room and try again with my laptop.

"Wyatt," I say. I shake him harder this time, because while I do feel bad about this, I also don't want to go back to my own room alone. I want to be here with him.

Wyatt opens one eye and peers up at me.

"What is it?" he asks, his voice thick and slurred with tiredness.

"We need to go over the pitch," I say. "Or I can do it myself."

He sits up and rubs his hands over his face and yawns. He shakes his head.

"No," he says. "I want to check everything too. Just give me a minute to go and splash some water on my face."

He goes off to the bathroom and I grab his laptop and get settled with it on my lap. I find the pitch and open it ready for him coming back. The toilet flushes and he comes back into the room looking a lot more awake.

"Ok, let's do this," he says, sitting back down beside me. "But first, there's something you should know. Now that you've woke me up, it'll take more than just reading this to knock me back out again, and I think, being that you woke me up, that should be your responsibility."

I lean over and kiss him.

"Ok," I say, and I wink at him. "I'll see what I can do."

CHAPTER 35

Serena

I'm dressed and ready to leave. I know I'm early, but I would rather be early than late. My laptop doesn't seem to have recovered from last night. It is still showing the green charging icon on the screen but that's it. It isn't actually charging, or it is charging, and its battery is full, but it still won't switch on. My first stop when I get back to the office will be to the IT department to see if they can fix it.

I have packed it away along with the rest of my things. Ruth managed to get us a late check out, so at least we don't have to lug our suitcases to the client's offices, but I'd rather be sorted now and then after the meeting I can just get changed and chill out until we need to leave for the airport.

I get up and go to the adjoining door. I don't suppose Wyatt is ready yet. I woke up well early this morning and after gathering my clothes from his balcony, I came back through to my own room to get ready. He was still asleep when I left him, his alarm set for an hour later than that. He's probably up by now though and at least I'll have someone to talk to if I go next door.

I tap on the door and push it open. I see the bathroom

door is open and I peer around towards the bed, half expecting Wyatt to still be in bed now that I've seen the bathroom isn't in use. I'm pleasantly surprised to see that actually, although he is sitting on the bed, he is ready.

"You're ready," I say with a smile.

"I could say the same about you," he replies.

"I woke up early and once I'm awake that's it," I say.

"I was actually just about to go downstairs and get a coffee. Do you want one?" Wyatt says. "I know we can make one, but that's just instant stuff. The one from downstairs is so much better."

"Sure. I'll have a latte please," I say.

Wyatt gets up and pats his pocket and then spins around searching. He spots what he was looking for – his cell phone and his wallet – and he puts them in his pocket.

"I won't be long," he says. "Oh, while I'm gone, do you mind doing me a favor?"

"No," I say. "What do you need?"

"Can you email Ruth the full pitch file. We'll be using her laptop for the presentation because it's got the best sound output. I have no idea how big Bellisario's conference room is, but if it's much bigger than ours, neither of our laptops would pack enough punch for everyone to hear the audio for the ad," he says.

"Yeah, I'll do that," I say. "No problem."

Wyatt gives me a quick kiss and then he rushes out of the room. I start to go back to my room to get my laptop when I remember it's still on the blink. I'll have to use Wyatt's laptop instead. I hope he has his passwords saved.

I open his laptop and the sign in screen comes up and then goes away, revealing his desktop without me having to sign in. So far so good. I click open his browser and go to his gmail account. I'm happy to find that yes, he does indeed save his passwords and I click use saved data and I'm in his email. I open a new message and type Ruth's name in the address bar and select her from the list that appears. I quickly attach the file and send a quick message saying everything is there and in order and all she needs to do is save the file and hit play when we say so. If I was emailing her off my laptop, I would be worried she would ignore me, but she will think this email is from Wyatt and so I'm confident that she will follow the instructions to the letter.

Her response pings in almost instantly. A simple enough email – 'got it'. I'm tempted to email her again, telling her to do something like make sure she is wearing yellow. Something I will be able to sit and enjoy but not something that will actually embarrass her, but I decide against it. Now isn't the time for messing with anyone who is going into that pitch, even if they are really only there to watch. I know Wyatt won't find it funny if Ruth asks him about it and he finds out I pulled a stunt like that before an important meeting. Still though, it's funny to imagine.

I close the email and the laptop before I can be any more tempted to do something to mess with her and when Wyatt comes back with the coffees, I have the giggles out of my system. I tell him I sent the presentation and that Ruth acknowledged receiving it.

We sit side by side on Wyatt's bed and drink our coffee – which he was right about; it is so much better than the instant stuff we could have made ourselves in the rooms – until it's time to leave the room. We go down in the elevator and meet Ruth in the lobby as arranged. She isn't exactly dancing with excitement to see me, but she does smile and wish me a good morning, a sentiment I return, so maybe she's mellowing a bit. Or maybe it's just her usual trick of being civil to me in front of Wyatt. Who knows. Who cares.

We all leave the hotel and head towards the client's head offices.

"Are you nervous?" Wyatt asks me, nodding down to where I'm twisting the fingers from both of my hands together in front of me.

"A little bit," I admit, although I would rather not show any fear in front of Ruth.

"Don't be," he says. "You know this stuff."

"I know," I say. "I'm not nervous about that. Like I know we have done the very best work we could have for the client, and I know what I need to say and all of that. I'm just always nervous when I have to speak in front of strangers in case I get all tongue tied and can't get my words out."

"Just pretend there's only Wyatt and me in the room with you," Ruth says. "You'll be fine."

"Thank you," I say, surprised that she's the one to be helping me.

I know she thaws a bit in front of Wyatt because she obviously doesn't want him to see her raging mean girl side, but still, that was a gesture that felt almost like someone being friendly. Maybe my asking her to have a drink last night finally made her thaw towards me. Maybe we can actually be friends now, or at least colleagues who don't actively dislike each other.

"That's good advice," Wyatt says and Ruth beams. I resist the urge to roll my eyes yet again. Some things will never change "Isn't there one about imagining the people you are talking to naked too?"

"Oh yeah. Imagining a room full of naked Italian men is going to do wonders for my concentration," I say with a laugh.

Wyatt frowns at me and I check quickly that Ruth isn't looking. She isn't and I blow him a kiss. He smiles and shakes his head. We reach the offices and step inside. I once more appreciate the wonder that is air conditioning as I step out of the heat and into the cool air of the lobby.

This place is the exact opposite of our hotel. It is grand, but there is nothing cosy or homely about it. Everything is monochrome and everything looks like it has sharp edges somehow, like if I was to sit down, I feel like I would somehow end up with a cut leg. Even the woman behind the desk in the lobby matches that sharp looking aesthetic. She's wearing a tight black skirt with a short white jumper (yes, a jumper in this heat) and she has black hair styled to within an inch of its life.

She says something in Italian and we all look at each other and then Wyatt steps forward.

"Sorry, do you speak English?" he asks.

"Of course," the woman replies in English with a slight accent. She taps one black lacquered nail on the desk as she speaks. "How can I help you?"

"We're from Smart Marketing Solutions. My name is Wyatt McAvoy. We have a meeting with Mr Bellisario," he says.

"Ah yes, he is expecting you," she says. She finally smiles and while it softens her face, she still looks like she is all hard edges. It's a most bizarre look and I keep blinking trying to see how she is doing it. She gets up and walks around from behind her desk. As I knew she would be, she is wearing stilettos that would be high enough to give the average person vertigo. "Follow me please."

She clacks off surprisingly quickly in her ankle breakers and the three of us follow her. She leads us through a maze of white walls and glass until we arrive at a door that she knocks on. A lone man sits in the room, and he looks up through the glass wall and beckons to the woman.

"Wyatt McAvoy and the marketing team from Smart Marketing Solutions are here," she says.

"Ah good, send them on in," the man says, standing up. The woman nods to us and moves aside, holding her arm out in gesture that means we should enter, and we go into the room. This room looks slightly less intimidating than the lobby.

The man who is greeting us is dressed in what, at first glance, appears to be casual clothes, but when you notice the name tags, you realize this man is wearing around twenty thousand dollars' worth of clothes. He wears them well, like someone used to luxury. From a distance, I thought he was about thirty, but now that he's closer, I can see where his tanned skin looks a little leathery and the feathery wrinkles around his eyes and I think he's nearer fifty, although he's in damned good shape.

CHAPTER 36

Serena

T he man introduces himself to Wyatt first and my suspicion is confirmed – this man is Roberto Bellisario, CEO of Bellisario's and a fashion legend. He reaches me next and smiles and extends his hand.

"Roberto Bellisario," he says.

"Hi Mr Bellisario. I'm Serena West," I say.

"Pleasure to meet you," he says. He winks at me. "And none of this Mr Bellisario stuff. Call me Roberto or Rob."

I nod in agreement, already knowing that I won't. Lastly, Ruth is greeted and then Mr Bellisario indicates that we should all sit down.

"If you guys want to get yourselves set up, go right ahead," he says. "I think everything you will need is here, but if not, Dante in the office next door will help you. I'm going to go and chase down some refreshments and I'll be back with a couple of others in around fifteen minutes."

"Thank you," all three of us say as he leaves.

Ruth is the first one to move. She busies herself setting up the laptop and I look over my notes in my notebook one more time.

"He's much more down to earth than I expected," I say quietly to Wyatt after I have reviewed as much as I can.

"Yeah, he always came across that way on the phone," Wyatt says. "But I wasn't sure if he would be the same in real life, but he seems like a decent guy."

"Yeah, I liked the vibe I got from him," I say. "I hope the others he brings back in with him are as nice as he is."

"Either way, it's him we have to impress most of all," Wyatt says.

I nod and then the conversation ends because Mr Bellisario is back. He is pushing a large trolley loaded with jugs of water and juice. He puts a jug of water, a jug of orange juice and a jug of what I assume is blackcurrant juice on the table near us and then he smiles and hands us a cup each.

We thank him. Wyatt pours himself a water and Ruth and I both have an orange juice. It's sweet and refreshing and I'm grateful for something to wet my throat. Mr Bellisario sits back down in his original seat and moments later, another three men appear and come and sit down around Mr Bellisario.

Mr Bellisario makes the introductions and then he says he is ready for us to begin whenever it suits us. Wyatt and I look at each other and he nods at me encouragingly.

I take one more drink of my juice and then I get to my feet and walk over to stand beside where the slides will appear on the screen. I introduce myself and then the first slide appears, and I begin to talk. I soon forget my nerves as I talk to Mr Bellisario and the others about what the modern fashionista is looking for in a brand and how we can show them that Bellisario's is the brand that can offer them all of that and more.

I talk for a good twenty minutes, but I keep a close eye on my audience, and at no point do any of them look bored. In fact, they look engaged, sitting forward in their seats, nodding along. One of them is even making notes on a sheet of paper. I think this is going really well and we're not even into the really good bit yet. Wyatt will be doing that side of the pitch – the part where he reveals the branding and the strategy for getting it out there along with the message that Bellisario's is a brand with quality, sustainable products that will take you from day to night and back again.

I finish speaking and smile around at the men.

"I will be taking questions at the end," I say. "In the meantime, I'm going to hand you over to Wyatt, who is going to explain to you all how we have rebranded the company and what strategies and gateways we will use to get your name out there as one of the major players to watch."

I sit back down, glad it went as well as I think it did, and Wyatt stands up and moves to where I was standing only a second ago. I glance at Ruth. She nods at me, a sign I hope that means I did good, and then her attention goes back to Wyatt and flicking through the slides.

I think I know Wyatt's part of the pitch as well as I knew my own and I'm practically mouthing the words along with him as he talks. I keep sneaking glances at Mr Bellisario and the others and they still seem to be completely engaged and focused. I hope that means it's a sure win for us. I don't want to jinx it, but it sure looks that way to me.

I keep watching and then I freeze as Ruth brings up the slide for the logo. I don't know what the hell that thing on the screen is, but it is most definitely not the logo that Wyatt and I designed for this brand. I can barely force myself to look away from the screen, but I do. I look at Mr Bellisario and the others. They have completely disengaged. They are sitting back in their seats and one of them is openly shaking his head.

I mean, honestly? I can't say I blame them. The logo on display is an absolute atrocity. I don't know what to do but I know I have to be the one to stop this. Wyatt is still talking, blissfully unaware of the garish monstrosity behind him on the screen and Ruth is oblivious to the fact that isn't the right logo.

"Umm," I say and then I clear my throat. "I'm sorry to interrupt."

Wyatt stops talking and looks at me in total shock.

"The slide that is currently displaying is wrong," I say.

Wyatt looks at it and his mouth drops open when he sees it. He turns immediately to Mr Bellisario and the others.

"My most sincere apologies gentlemen. I have no idea how that got in there, but I assure you, that is not the logo we have designed for you," he says.

"Then where is that one?" Mr Bellisario asks.

Wyatt shakes his head, as lost as the rest of us. He walks over to Ruth's laptop and flicks backwards and forwards a few screens but there is no other logo. This monstrosity hasn't just been added in, it has somehow replaced the real logo.

"Forgive me for speaking so bluntly, but in my opinion, it seems that you designed us that logo and your associate here saw our reaction to it and tried to save the pitch," he says.

"I assure you that's not true, Sir. I would be embarrassed to have designed that thing," Wyatt says.

My mind is racing. How can we prove this was never their logo? An idea comes to me, and I flick back through my notebook until I find what I'm looking for.

"Mr Bellisario. Umm Roberto," I say. All eyes focus on me, and I want the ground to open up and swallow me, but I have to show them this. "This is obviously an early draft and a very rough sketch, but this here is the actual logo we worked on for you. As you can see, it is in my notebook pages back with your brief and other things. It hasn't just been inserted there today."

I hand my notebook over to Mr Bellisario. He looks at it and he gives me a small smile and nods.

"This is much more like it," he says, poking the design gently with his finger.

The others agree and then they pass my notebook back to me.

"Let's carry on," Mr Bellisario says. "If we are happy with everything else, you can send the final draft of that logo over for our consideration after the pitch."

CHAPTER 37

Wyatt

I 'm so angry I could smash this whole room up, but I keep my game face on and remain professional as I go through the rest of the pitch. I present the pitch properly – the perfectionist in me won't let me do anything else – but it kind of feels like a waste of my time at this point as it's obvious we've lost this client before we ever even had them.

I can't believe Serena has let this happen. The number of times she double checked the pitch and it still ended up in there says to me that somehow, she thought that was the right logo, which says to me she thought it was an ok logo and didn't think it was ugly. That is so much worse than her just not knowing it was in there. For her to think that ugly ass thing suited the Bellisario's brand really worries me.

As much as I love spending time with Serena and as much as I want her in my life, I know I'm going to have to fire her. I can't have this kind of mistake happening at this level. This deal was going to be worth billions of dollars to the company, and I can't just let it get thrown away. I would be more than happy to still date Serena, but I doubt she will want to speak to me after I have fired her.

I still have to do it though. I accept that it's partly my fault. We both have been flirting and carrying on a bit, but I really thought we had this thing nailed. And yes, I was encouraging the flirting, but I am not the one who fucked up. I thought Serena was better than this – that's my major mistake.

I wonder absently if this is going to go down better or worse with Craig and Martin. Firing her or fucking her. Which will cause the biggest ructions. Maybe they'll end up hearing about both. I hope Serena is mature enough to separate business and pleasure because if she tells her dad I fucked her and then fired her, it's not going to look good for me and no amount of explaining would make Martin see me as anything other than a right bastard after that.

My pitch finally comes to an end, and I have never been more relieved to finish a pitch than I am with that one.

"Do you have any questions gentlemen?" I ask.

I'm almost certain there won't be any. They don't need to ask questions of a firm they aren't going to hire about a campaign they aren't going to use. I'm surprised then when one of them asks me a question about social media and whether I think using influencers is a good idea.

I explain that it has its good points – more people will see the brand being the chief one - but that it also has it's not so good points. Most of the people who will see the brand through the Instagram type influencer are teenagers with no disposable income and I also explain that it makes the brand less exclusive if it looks like they have to give stuff away to get Z listers to wear the brand. Blogs on the other hand, I explain, are more credible and their readers tend to be adults with money to spend.

We go back and forth a little bit about how it all works, and they seem satisfied with the answers. They ask me a couple more questions and then Roberto asks Serena a couple of questions, all of which she handles impeccably. How did this polished girl who knows so much about this brand get that logo thing so wrong?

"OK, thank you for your time, Wyatt, Serena, Ruth," Roberto says, nodding at each of us in turn. "My colleagues and I would like to have a discussion about your services. Would it be rude of me to ask you to stay until after the discussion just in case we would like anything clarified for us?"

"No, that's not rude at all. We are perfectly happy to wait," I say.

Somehow, it feels like we might still have a chance at this. I don't know how but surely they wouldn't go this far just to be polite. If they wanted to be polite, they would say they'd let us know then send a no thank you email in a day or two in my experience.

I don't know which way this meeting is going to go anymore but I still know what I have to do, and I want to get it over with quickly before I can change my mind, because even if we get away with it this time, I can't risk it happening again and if I have to double check even the simplest little things that Serena does, then what's the point in having her around? I may as well just do the work myself.

Roberto and the others leave the conference room and I turn to Ruth.

"Would you pop out and get us some coffees please?" I ask.

"Isn't it a little hot for coffee?" she asks. "We've got juice and water here."

"And you are free to drink either of those when you return. In the meantime, I would like you to fetch me a coffee please," I say, barely keeping my temper.

Ruth seems to sense that this isn't the time to argue with me. I mean she is right – it's not the weather for coffee, but I don't want an audience when I fire Serena. I owe her that much that this will be dealt with quietly and privately. I watch her leave the room and the second the door closes, I turn to Serena.

"What the fuck were you thinking?" I demand.

"What?" she says, looking taken aback that I'm shouting at her.

"That fucking logo. I don't remember it even being a thing we drafted up let along anything I would have approved. How the hell did it get left in the presentation for the client?" I demand.

"It didn't," she says. "Or at least it didn't get put in any version I saw. I have no idea where that came from, I swear it."

"So, you're saying I put it there, are you? That I decided it would be fun to sabotage my own company and make myself look like an idiot in front of other people?" I ask.

"I'm not saying that at all. What I am saying is that I didn't put that slide in there and I don't know how it got there," Serena says.

She seems so genuine and God how I want to believe her. I almost do believe her. But there has only been me and her putting the pitch together and I know it wasn't me so by the process of elimination, it has to be her. Right?

"Ok. Let's pretend for a second that it just magically put itself in there should we? Why didn't you spot it before you sent the slides over?" I ask.

"Why didn't you?" Serena fires back.

"Excuse me?" I roar, conscious of being in a client's building, but unable to keep my voice down for a moment.

"Why didn't you spot it?" Serena says again. "We went through it together last night. If I should have seen it, so should you. But I'll tell you why you didn't see it. For the same reason as I didn't. It wasn't fucking there."

"So, it must have been on your copy of the pitch then," I say.

"Nope. I think I would have remembered that," she says.

I'm starting to rant. I can't help it. This is so much harder than I thought it would be. For starters, I didn't expect Serena to deny all knowledge of this, and I definitely didn't expect her to challenge me on why I didn't see it either. She has once more thrown me for a loop, but I'm so mad I don't know what to do with it at the moment.

"Wait," she says, interrupting me mid rant. She looks excited suddenly and she jumps to her feet and starts pacing the floor. "We both looked through that presentation last night, right?" She stops pacing and looks at me and it seems like she's waiting for an answer. I nod and she nods back to me and then starts pacing again. As she paces, she goes on. "And then this morning, you asked me to send the presentation slides to Ruth. My laptop isn't working remember. I sent it from your laptop off your email. I sent the file we both checked. That means ..."

She trails off and I finish the sentence for her.

"Ruth messed up," I say. "Not you."

Serena nods and pours herself a glass of the purple-colored juice. She sits back down and sips the juice angrily. She has every right to be angry. I have jumped to a conclusion that was wrong and I wouldn't hear her when she tried to explain. Fuck me, I have fucked up here. I won't make that same mistake again though.

For all I want to believe Serena, at the same time, Ruth has worked for me for a long time, and I can't think of any reason why she would do this. Even if the logo slide was missing, which I know it wasn't, she wouldn't just take it upon herself to design that crap and chuck it in there. I have to make sure there's some truth to what Serena is saying before Ruth gets back. At this point, I don't know what to make of anything, but I guess it's possible that Serena changed the logo before sending Ruth the email and then lied about it. I don't see why she would do that, but I also don't see why Ruth would change out the logo. Neither of those options make sense but I can't think of a third one.

CHAPTER 38

Wyatt

I get my cell phone out and open my email account. I find the email Serena said she sent and the reply she said Ruth sent. All good so far. I open the attachment and flick through the slides, and I soon see the logo slide – with the correct logo on it. Serena was right. I still don't know fully what happened, but whatever it was happened after Serena had done her part on the slides and after they were out of her hands. What the actual fuck was Ruth thinking? And what the actual fuck was I thinking to go off on Serena like that without even hearing her side of the story first? God what a fucking mess this is turning out to be.

There is one silver lining though, one thing I am so glad about in all of this. I don't have to fire Serena now, and I hope I can make it up to her that I overreacted and shouted at her. I am also a bit gutted though. I really don't want to lose Ruth either. She has something against Serena, I know that much, but other than that, she has always been an excellent worker and I have always trusted her. Still, if I have to lose one of them, I will choose to lose Ruth every time. Maybe that's not the correct professional decision to make, but I would make it all the same without hesitation. Sorry Ruth. You're good, but you're no Serena.

I don't have to wait long before Ruth is back. She has two cups of coffee, one of which she hands to me and the other one she gives to Serena. That must have irked her, having to get Serena a cup of coffee. I don't even know if Serena wanted a coffee, but she's thanked Ruth for it and now she's sipping at it so whatever. I pick mine up and blow on the surface and then I take a drink. It's good and I drink again. I'm only prolonging the inevitable, but it's nice to just act like everything is perfectly normal for a moment. Ruth is pouring herself a cup of water. I let her sit down and have a drink and then I can't put it off any longer.

"Ruth, I need to see your laptop," I say.

"Why?" she asks.

"I think you know why," I say. "I want to see what time that logo slide was inserted into our presentation and from what IP address it was added."

I know I can do the first thing and if the time matches a time after Ruth received it, that will convince me. I have no idea if the IP address thing is even possible, but it sounds good, and I'm hoping it will make Ruth confess which would make this whole thing easier all around.

"You don't need to do that," Ruth says. "Not from my laptop anyway. I didn't add or change anything, I just played the thing and clicked when they needed moving on."

"Then you'll have no problem with me looking," I say. Ruth starts to object again, and I hold up my hand for silence. "Ruth, I'm not asking you anymore, I am telling you. The laptop is company property and I want to look at it please. This will not bode well for you if you force me to wait until we get home and go to the IT department to get into it instead of you typing the password in yourself now."

Ruth sighs and makes a show of pulling her laptop towards herself like this is just a minor inconvenience to her, but as she types her password in, I can see her fingers are shaking. She pushes the laptop towards me, and I go to take it, but before I can, Ruth bursts into tears.

"Fine," she says. "You got me, ok? I added that slide in there."

"What? Why?" I demand. "Why would you try and sabotage the company? I don't get it."

"It wasn't about the company. I didn't think that part of it through. I was trying to sabotage her," Ruth says. She points to Serena. "For years I have been by your side, organizing your life, helping you, going the extra mile for you, showing you that I have your back one hundred percent. I always contended myself by telling myself you were enjoying being single, but one day that might change, and when it did, maybe you would think of the person who had been loyal to you for all those years. And then she came along, and you soon forgot about the single life and about me, didn't you? I had to do something to make you get rid of her. You were meant to end up with me, not some random kid."

Serena's jaw drops open as Ruth makes her confession and I'm sure my own expression is similar to hers. I don't like the implication of Serena being a kid, but I know Ruth is just lashing out, trying to hurt me like I have somehow unintentionally hurt her and so I let it go and when I speak to her, my voice is soft and kind. She is already broken. She doesn't need me to yell at her. And I can't deny the truth of everything else she has said about how she has always been there for me and the company until Serena arrived on the scene.

"Ruth, you know I have to fire you right?" I ask. She nods and sniffs miserably. "You are fired as of right now. Please go and catch your flight home and I will have someone contact you about collecting your things from the office."

Ruth nods but she makes no movement and I stand up myself.

"Come on. I'm going to escort you out in case you try to make any trouble here," I say. I turn to Serena. "If Mr Bellisario or the others come back, answer any questions they have and if they're ready for me, tell them I will be back in a moment ok."

She nods and I beckon to Ruth. She picks up her purse and follows miserably behind me. We get outside and I stop walking and face Ruth.

"I'm sorry it came to this," I say. "Until the last few weeks, you were my best employee – and a good friend. Someone I could rely on."

"I'm sorry too," Ruth says with a miserable sniff.

"Cell phone," I say and hold my hand out.

"Huh?" Ruth says. It seems to take her a minute to realize her cell phone is actually a company cell phone. A panicked expression crosses her face when she realizes the truth of that. "Can I hand it in when I come to collect my things? I won't use it unless it's an emergency, but I haven't brought my other cell phone and the thought of travelling with no cell phone scares me."

I watch her as she speaks, and she seems genuine. I think it would make me at the very least nervous to fly without being in contact with anyone too. I nod.

"I'm trusting you not to abuse the favor," I say.

"I won't. I promise. Thank you," she says.

She walks away without another word, and I allow her that dignity. I watch until she is out of sight and then I turn to go back into the building, but I decide there are a couple of quick calls I need to make first, not least to the VP of the company to warn him about Ruth in case she turns up for work as normal.

I hurry back outside and make my first call. When the call is answered, I cross my fingers and begin to speak.

"Hi. I have a current booking under the name Smart Marketing Solutions. We have a room on the seventh floor and two adjoining rooms on the eighth floor. We're meant to be checking out today, but I wondered if you had availability for the two adjoining rooms for an extra night?" I ask.

"Let me check that for you Sir," the hotel receptionist replies.

I hear the clack, clack sound of her nails on the keyboard and then she speaks again.

"That's just the two adjoining rooms? The other room is to be checked out today?" she says.

"Yes," I agree.

More clacking and then she's back again.

"Yes Sir, I have that availability," she says. "Would you like me to book the rooms for you?"

"Yes please," I say, a swirl of excitement rolling around my stomach as I answer her. I wait a few moments while her clacking fingers work their magic and then she's talking to me again.

"OK, that's all arranged Sir, and the additional charge has been added to your original payment method," she says.

"Thank you," I say, and end the call.

CHAPTER 39

Wyatt

I'm hopeful that the extra night's stay in the beautiful hotel in Rome will help Serena stop being mad at me a bit quicker. Next, I call the airline and book us two first class seats on a flight tomorrow and finally, I get around to calling the VP of my company. I explain what's happened and tell him that if Ruth comes in without an appointment to collect her things, she is to be sent away. I say if he hears from her to arrange the collection or if not to leave it until I'm back. I tell him that we're going to be here another night and then I end the call before he can ask why. It's none of his business and I would be within my rights to say that but he's not just an employee, he's a friend and I know he wouldn't be asking to pry, he would just be making conversation, so I don't want to have to be rude to him and he will know instantly if I lie or try to hide something from him.

My calls made, I know it's time for me to go back inside and face the music with Serena. I think I can safely say this is the first time ever that I'm on my way to see Serena and I am not looking forward to it. I'm going to have to eat some mega humble pie.

If she was just an employee, I would give her a genuine apology and that would be it because under the circumstances, no one could say I jumped to a strange conclusion, but I feel like as someone Serena is in a relationship with, I should have been much quicker to give her the benefit of the doubt, despite what things looked like.

I go back to the conference room. Serena is still alone in there. I go and sit down beside her and pour myself some water.

"Has anyone been in with any questions?" I ask, deciding to start off on safe ground.

"No," Serena says. "Did Ruth go easy?"

"Surprisingly, yes," I say. "If you're wondering why I was gone so long, I was making a few phone calls. I've changed our flights home and booked us an extra night at the hotel, just the two of us."

For this first time since all of this kicked off, Serena smiles and I feel like it's going to be ok between us after all.

"Is that your way of saying you're sorry for not only doubting my word but for yelling at me too?" she asks.

"Yes," I say bluntly, and she actually laughs. I dare to smile at her. "I really am sorry Serena. I should have known you wouldn't have done something like that and that if you had, you wouldn't have lied about it."

"Apology accepted," Serena says. "I can see how it looked and I can see why you didn't even consider Ruth at first. But if anything like that ever happens again and I tell you I didn't do something, I would appreciate it if you at least had the decency to give me the benefit of the doubt."

"I will. I definitely will," I say, and I mean it. I'm getting a second chance and I won't screw that up.

"Then you're forgiven," Serena says. "And I would kiss

you, but you can pretty much guarantee if I did, the moment our lips touch, the clients would come back in."

She's barely finished the sentence and Mr Bellisario appears in front of the glass wall.

"Told you," Serena says, and we look at each other and try not to laugh as Mr Bellisario comes back in.

He smiles at us, and I smile back. He sits down in the seat he recently vacated.

"Thank you for waiting," he says. He seems to notice Ruth is gone. "Do we need to wait for your other associate?"

"No, it's fine," I say. "Ruth isn't really part of the campaign, she's my PA."

Was my PA, not is, but I'm not about to tell Mr Bellisario that I've fired her. He seems to accept the explanation that she doesn't need to be here, and he smiles again.

"I expected there to be questions, but it seems you two explained everything well enough that even my social media averse CFO understands the need for using it for marketing purposes," he says. "I have never met anyone who could make that man see the good side of social media and honestly, that alone would have been reason to hire you, but of course I couldn't base my decision on that alone in reality. But everything considered, I would like to hire you to do the marketing you discussed in your pitch for the fee we agreed on prior to the meeting. I can have the paperwork completed and sent over to your office by the end of the day if that works for you? And, of course, if you would still like to work with us."

"We would of course love to work with you," I say. "And that sounds great. Serena and I will be back in the office at some point the day after tomorrow and I will get everything started for you then."

Mr Bellisario stands up and I take it as our cue to leave. I stand up and Serena does the same thing. We both shake hands with Mr Bellisario and then I grab Ruth's laptop and we leave the conference room.

We walk out of the building, the picture of calmness, like we land billion dollar deals every day. We leave the building and turn back towards the hotel and walk calmly away. And then, as soon as we are out of sight of the building, as one, we both cheer. I fist pump the air and Serena does a little happy dance. I pull her into my arms and kiss her.

"Separate, we're both damned good at this job. Together, we are unstoppable," I say.

"And to think you only gave me a job because my Uncle Craig would never have let you forget it if you said no to him," she says.

I laugh and shake my head.

"I never thought of it that way, but yeah you're at least partially right," I admit.

We're back at the hotel but as we head for the door, Serena stops me.

"I know it's cheesy, but before we go in can we please go and do the coin in the fountain thing?" she says.

"Of course," I laugh. "Most tourist things are cheesy. It doesn't mean they aren't fun though. Do you have some euros?"

Serena nods. "Yeah, I got some in the airport on the way out."

We walk over to the fountain and turn our backs on it. We both hold a coin in our hands.

"Don't forget to make a wish," Serena says.

I don't think that's how it works but what the hell. I close my eyes, throw my coin over my shoulder, and wish that Serena and I can spend the rest of our lives together. I open my eyes and smile at her, and we sit down on the low wall around the fountain.

"So, what did you wish for?" she asks as we watch the water flow.

"I can't tell you or it won't come true," I say.

"That's a good point, you'd better not risk it," she says. Her voice is serious, but her eyes are playful, and I love the way she looks in that moment, the mist of the water behind her. She must be able to feel my eyes on her.

"What?" she says, self-conscious all of a sudden. "Do I have something on my face?"

"Only your cute little nose," I say.

She rolls her eyes and I laugh.

"I was just thinking how beautiful you are and how amazing you look with that backdrop," I say. "And that's the truth."

"I already forgave you for being a dick earlier. You can stop this now," Serena says with a laugh.

"I'll never stop telling you how beautiful you are," I say.

I lean forward and kiss her, conscious of the fact that we are in a very public spot so I can't kiss her deeply how I would like to. I have to settle for a soft and gentle kiss, a promise of more to come beneath the surface of it.

"Should we go up to the rooms and get out of our work clothes and go out for a nice dinner?" I say,

Serena stands up and I do too, and we start to head back towards the hotel.

"I have a better idea," Serena says.

"Go on then, spill it," I say when she doesn't go any further.

"How about we go up to the rooms, get out of our work clothes and order room service," she says. "Then you know, we wouldn't need to worry about getting back into other clothes if you get my drift."

Oh, I get her drift. I very much get her drift.

"You were right. Your plan is better," I say. "Let's do that instead."

CHAPTER 40

Serena

We head back to the hotel and as we walk across the lobby, I can feel a lovely warm glow inside of me. All in all, it's been an eventful but amazing day. In this one day, Ruth's true colors have come out and she is now out of the picture, meaning I won't have her attitude and glares to put up with at work any longer. Mind you, in some ways I will miss her – she definitely kept me alert. We won a massive contract that was partly due to me for my work on the campaign and also for having the foresight to show Mr Bellisario the correct logo design with the proof that we hadn't just come up with it on the spot. And as if all of that wasn't enough, I am now getting to spend an extra night in the most beautiful city I've ever seen with the man I am very quickly falling for.

What more could a girl possibly ask for? Oh yes. Room service and red-hot sex and both of those are very much on the cards for later. Tonight is going to be even better than today has been if I have my way and it looks like I am very much about to get my way.

The elevator comes and we step into the car. A few others

get in, but that doesn't stop Wyatt from taking my hand in his. I love that we can do that just like any normal couple now that we don't have Ruth watching our every move. We get to our floor and make our way along the hallway.

Wyatt stops at his room door, and I automatically keep walking until I realize Wyatt hasn't released my hand and he's laughing and then I laugh too. There's no reason not to just go in through his door now and if I need anything from my room, I can use the adjoining door. There's no reason to hide this anymore. Really, Wyatt could have just kept one room for tonight, but then we would have had to wait to start our night of fun while I went next door and gathered up my things to bring through, and I'm glad I don't have to do that until tomorrow now. Wyatt probably didn't even realize that I was mostly packed. Plus, he might have thought it was a little bit presumptuous although I don't know why – it's not like we don't stay over at each other's places at home.

As soon as we are in the room and the door has been closed behind us, Wyatt reaches for me and pulls me into his arms and starts kissing me. My body responds to his kiss as always, my clit tingling and my pussy clenching in anticipation of what's to come. I press my lips against Wyatt's and battle his tongue with mine.

I feel as though I don't have a care in the world while I'm locked in Wyatt's arms and our bodies are pressed together like this. My only concern is that I want to feel Wyatt's hands all over me, his tongue all over. I want to feel him inside of me. I can feel his cock pressing against my stomach now and it's no good there – I need to feel him inside of me and I want him in there right now, but I also want this to last.

We are edging towards the bed as we kiss, our clothes coming off. We break our kiss apart long enough to get our clothes off and then we come back together, and our kiss is even more frantic, even more hungry, than it was before. I want to devour Wyatt and I want to be devoured by him. Our hands are all over each other's bodies, caressing and stroking.

We reach the bed and Wyatt pulls his mouth from mine but before he can say or do anything else, I have an idea and I gently push him onto the bed. He lands in a sitting position, and I motion for him to scoot backwards which he does, sitting with his legs stretched out in front of him. I climb on the bed and straddle him. I wrap my arms around him, and I kiss him lightly on the lips, running my lips over his, enjoying the lightly tickling sensation it causes in my mouth and lips.

"Lay back," I whisper, releasing Wyatt from my arms.

He eagerly does as I say and when he's lying flat on his back, I crawl forwards until I have completely cleared his body and then I turn around and crawl back. I position myself so that my pussy is at Wyatt's mouth and then I grab his hard cock in my fist and put it into my mouth and then I begin to suck on it. Wyatt doesn't need any instructions. Even as he moans his pleasure, he is grabbing my hips and licking my clit. The vibration of his moan against my clit feels amazing, and I feel myself already inching towards my climax.

I let Wyatt set the pace. When his flicking tongue becomes feather light against me, teasing me, I copy him on his cock, my tongue gently licking over his tip. When he gives me some relief, putting pressure on my clit and sending me closer to my orgasm, I do the same for him, drawing him into my mouth and sucking hard.

I'm so close to coming when Wyatt stops moving my clit from side to side in a delicious rhythm and gently blows on it. It feels good but I know what he's doing – he's holding my orgasm back, teasing me again. I start to do the same to him, but then I take his length back into my mouth.

I'm done teasing him now. I want to make him come hard

in my mouth and then I will get mine. I lift myself slightly so that my pussy is no longer in reach of Wyatt's tongue, teasing him at that end instead of the other end, and then I go wild on his cock, sucking hard, my head bobbing up and down quickly. One hand is fisted around the base of Wyatt's cock, matching my thrusting head, and making sure his full length gets some attention. The other hand cups his balls and caresses them.

I don't stop and even when I feel Wyatt straining to reach my pussy again, I don't move closer to him. I just keep working him. I feel him relax beneath me and stop trying to fight me and it spurs me on. I up my pace even more, using my tongue to add pressure and I hear Wyatt make a strangled 'arghh' sound and then my mouth is filled with his spunk, and I swallow it, savoring the taste of him and sucking on him after I have swallowed, making sure I get every last drop.

When I'm sure he is done, I release his cock from my mouth and fist, and I push myself up onto all fours and then I lower my pussy again, so that it's once more nice and close to Wyatt's face. He moans as he starts to lick me again. It doesn't take much to get me back to the edge – I barely really left it – and when Wyatt pushes his tongue inside of my pussy it's too much for me to take and my orgasm explodes through my body.

I feel my muscles tightening and a shiver of pleasure goes through my body. My clit tingles and pulses and aches for more. My pussy clenches and my juices run freely from me into Wyatt's waiting mouth. My nipples tingle and grow and for a moment, my breath catches in my throat as my whole body pulses with pleasure. It's almost painful, but not enough to take away from the pleasure. It's sweet pain, exquisite torture, and I relish every second of it.

When I can breathe again, I unhook my leg from over

Wyatt's face, and I lay down beside him. His fingers find mine and we lay like that for a moment until we have our breaths back. I sit up after a few minutes.

"Well, as nice as that was, it didn't do much for my hunger. I'm starving," I say.

Wyatt laughs softly beside me and then he sits up and picks up the room service menu from his bedside cabinet and hands it to me. I look through it, my mouth watering at all the delicious looking choices.

"I think I'm going to have the chicken penne arrabbiata," I say after a few minutes.

I hand the menu to Wyatt who looks at it for a moment and then picks up the receiver of the land line telephone and calls down to reception. He orders my penne, carbonara for himself and a bottle of wine for us to share.

I am so hungry, and I know I'll get impatient just sitting waiting, so I stand up.

"I'm going to take a shower while we wait for the food," I say. "Can I go in yours or do you want to go in yours and I'll go in mine?"

"We could both go in mine," Wyatt says with a grin and a raised eyebrow.

I laugh and shake my head.

"We'll never be out in time for our food coming," I say.

"Fair enough," Wyatt says. "You go on. I'll follow you in. Like as in once you've finished."

CHAPTER 41

Serena

I wake up and look at my watch. Fuck. It's after ten o'clock and we're going to miss our flight. Wyatt is still fast asleep beside me, and I reach over and shake him.

"Wyatt, Wyatt, wake up," I say. He makes a mm sound, but he doesn't open his eyes. "Wake up. We've slept in."

This gets his attention, and he opens his eyes and rubs his hand across them. I sit up and throw the covers back. Wyatt sits up and reaches for his cell phone while I rush towards the adjoining door.

"I'll shower in my room. It'll be quicker," I say. "Then we can both be ready together instead of you having to wait for me."

"Serena, come back to bed," Wyatt says.

"But ..." I start.

"But nothing," Wyatt says, cutting me off. "It's ten past ten pm. We haven't overslept; we just fell asleep early."

"Oh," I say, my hand falling away from the door handle of the adjoining room. I remember now. We ate our food and then we both said how stuffed we were and how we couldn't move. I remember telling myself I was just going to close my eyes for a few minutes and then I would feel better. And yes, that had been at about eight o'clock.

I start back towards the bed and Wyatt gets up.

"I'm going to the bathroom," he says.

I nod and get back into bed. It's warm and comfy but I think it'll be a while before I can sleep now because essentially, I have just had a lovely long nap. Wyatt comes back into the room and gets into bed beside me. I turn to face him.

"So," he says, smiling at me. "Should we finish what we started earlier?"

I smile back at him and nod. He drops a pillow on the floor beside the bed and I frown, confused. His smile disappears and when he looks at me, he is intense, the lust all over his face and when he speaks, his voice is dripping with both lust and authority, and I feel a fluttering in my stomach and in my pussy at the sound of it.

"Get down on the ground," he commands. "Kneel on the pillow and put your palms flat on the wall."

I don't move immediately, and Wyatt raises an eyebrow.

"Now," he says louder and with more authority. I feel my pussy flooding with heat and liquid, and I jump up and almost run to his side of the bed to do what he says. This is new and I feel like it's going to be so fucking hot.

I kneel on the pillow and lean forward and put my palms flat on the wall like he asked me too. Or to be precise, commanded me too. The thought brings another rush of warm wetness in my pussy.

The position I'm in leaves my body stretched out, my ass in the air and absently, I wonder if I'm dripping on the carpet. I hear the rustling of the sheets as Wyatt stands up and I don't' care if I am dripping or not, I just want Wyatt inside of me now. I then feel a puff of air over the backs of my legs as Wyatt drops another pillow on the ground behind me. He gets down onto the pillow and then his hands are on my inner thighs, and he forces my legs further apart.

"That's better," he says. "Now Serena, you know I am not a morning person."

"It's not morning though," I remind him.

I feel him shifting and then I feel his chest against my back, the fronts of his legs against the backs of mine. He envelopes me in his warmth, but he isn't finished with the dominating side of himself yet. I have to admit I am far from finished with that side of him myself. He definitely needs to come out to play more often. I'm going to have to start being a bad girl a bit more regularly, I think.

He grabs my hair at the nape of my neck and winds the length of it around his fist. He pulls on it, pulling my head back and I whimper at the feeling. The stinging sensation on my scalp is painful, but somewhere it melds with the pleasure and the anticipation of what's to come and it makes me feel good, like I can handle anything Wyatt throws at me.

"Don't fucking answer me back," he growls in my ear.

I feel his breath tickling my neck and a pulse of lust goes through me.

"Ok, I won't," I say.

He releases my hair and I sigh in relief.

"That's better," he says.

"Now as I said, I am not a morning person, and I am going to punish you for waking me up for no reason," he says.

He has barely gotten the sentence out of his mouth, and he is inside of me in one stinging thrust, his huge cock slamming into me with no warning, filling me all the way. I cry out and Wyatt thrusts into me again.

He is relentless in his thrusts. Each one is hard and deep, and I barely have time to take a breath between them. I'm not sure if I'm supposed to like it or not, but holy fuck I do like it.

I clench my pussy, tightening it around Wyatt's cock and I hear the sharp intake of breath from behind me and I smile a little bit to myself. Wyatt might be in control in one way, but I am definitely in control in another.

He's working himself up into quite a frenzy and although I didn't think I would be able to orgasm from penetration alone, he is working me into quite a frenzy too. If he thinks this is going to stop me from waking him up early again, he is very much mistaken. It is only encouraging me to do it every morning. I'm not sure Wyatt quite understands what the term punishment means because he said this is a punishment and it feels like heaven.

Another hard thrust into me and this one rubs his cock across my g spot and that feeling inside of me pushes me over the edge. I cry out, screaming Wyatt's name as I come hard. My elbows collapse and start to bend and the only thing stopping me from hitting the ground on my face is Wyatt's hands on my hips. He pulls me back and forth as he keeps thrusting and pleasure keeps flying around my body leaving me gasping for air and my body floppy.

He pulls me right back one more time and I feel him orgasm. His fingers dig into my hips, and I think that slightly painful grip is the only thing that stops me from passing out as another wave of pleasure crashes over me and I go rigid. I can't breathe. I can't think. I can't see. I can only ride this wave of intoxicating ecstasy.

It starts to fade, and I come back to myself. I can see again, and I can breathe again, and I'm panting, trying to get myself under some sort of control. Wyatt moans my name and then he slips out of me and moves back onto his knees. He pulls me with him, and I sit on his lap, wrapped up in his arms. I lean back against his chest, and I can feel it rising and falling fast as he pants, and I can feel his heartbeat racing.

I reach up with one hand and put it behind his neck, pulling his face down to mine. I press my lips against his and we kiss deeply and lovingly, and we only break apart when neither of us can get enough air. I slump against Wyatt, sated and content in his arms.

I don't know how long has passed, but I'm starting to doze off when Wyatt moves beneath me, and I wake up with a start. We are still on the ground.

"Sorry," Wyatt says as he gently lifts me off his lap. "I have a cramp in my leg."

He gets up and massages the cramp out of his muscle. I watch him for a moment, drinking in his beautiful body and then I force my aching body to stand up. I gather the pillows and put them back on the bed and then I get on to the bed on Wyatt's side and shuffle across to my side. Wyatt gets in beside me.

I lay on my side facing Wyatt and Wyatt lays on his stomach, his face turned towards me. He smiles at me, and I smile back sleepily.

"So now you know what happens if you wake me up before I have to be up," Wyatt says with a twinkle in his eye.

"Oh God, don't say that" I say with a soft laugh. "Neither of us will ever sleep again."

He laughs.

"Fair point," he says.

He reaches across the gap between us, and I think he wants to hold my hand, but his searching hand moves past my fingers and the next thing I know, he has two fingers between my lips, one on either side of my swollen clit. I hiss slightly, sucking air in through my teeth, as my clit pulses painfully. It is so tender from everything we have already done tonight, but his touch has already awakened my lust for him, and my clit is pulsing with desire despite the pain.

He starts off gentle, rubbing me with a barely-there touch until my clit settles down. After a moment or two, the intense pain has become the usual intense amazing feeling that comes with my clit being touched. Wyatt must feel my body relaxing because he seems to know that I'm no longer hurting, and he ups the intensity of his touch. I bend my top leg and rest on the flat of my foot, so I'm more open to Wyatt's touch.

This time, he isn't massaging my clit. He keeps his fingers one on either side of it and he scissors them, creating a sensation not unlike a heartbeat where each strike sends a flood of pleasure through my pussy. Just when I get used to the sensation, he changes it up. His fingers still scissor on me, in and out, squeezing and releasing, but now they also move backwards and forwards, rubbing against the sides of my clit as they scissor in and out.

The new sensation pushes me over the edge, and I come before I even realize I'm on the brink of an orgasm. I feel a shudder go through my whole body and I close my eyes and float away on wave after wave of gentle pleasure. Each wave is more intense than the one before it, and I'm sure that I can't take any more of this, but more keeps on coming and I keep on taking it.

I can feel my face screwing up as though I'm in pain and my lungs and throat burn where I try and fail to breath. My muscles have all gone tight and I can't move any of my body. A small whimper leaves my lips as yet another wave of indescribable pleasure crashes over me and then I feel Wyatt's fingers slip away from me and my rigid muscles turn to jelly, and I flop face first into the pillow.

I still can't breathe, only now it's because of the pillow in my face, and I turn my head slightly and find that I can breathe perfectly well, and then Wyatt's lips rub over mine and I smile, and I enjoy the coming down feeling, the heavy but contented feeling in my body, mind and soul. I feel myself starting to fall asleep once I have my breath back and I shuffle closer to Wyatt and snuggle up against him. He puts his arm around me and holds me close and I don't think I have ever felt as good as I do in this moment.

CHAPTER 42
Serena

I look up from my computer when there is a knock on my office door.

"Come in," I say.

The door opens and I feel my jaw drop with shock. Standing in the doorway to my office is the last person I expected to see there. Ruth.

"Ruth? What the hell are you doing here?" I say, not even trying to hide my surprise at seeing her here.

"Well, after the way Wyatt treated me, I thought I would come back and blow the place up. And I couldn't resist stopping by the office of my favorite associate to brag about my evil master plan first," she says.

I'm not sure whether she's joking or not and my expression must show it because Ruth snorts out a laugh and shakes her head.

"Come on Serena. I'm not that bat shit crazy," she says. She walks towards me, and I resist the urge to flinch back, but she doesn't try anything, she just sits down opposite me. Once she's sitting down, I feel better. I didn't like the idea of her towering over me whether she's joking about being crazy or not.

"Anyway, no need to shit a brick or call security or anything. I'm here to collect my things," she says. "With Wyatt's knowledge."

"Do you have another job lined up?" I ask, trying to move the conversation away from Wyatt before it goes somewhere even more awkward than this is.

It's only been three days since Wyatt fired her, but a good PA never struggles to find work and I'm not surprised when Ruth nods.

"Yes, I have a place at Stoddard and Keel," she says. "I start work on Monday as the PA for Mrs Keel."

Stoddard and Keel is one of Smart Marketing Solution's competitors, but there's really nothing Ruth can do there to sabotage Wyatt or the firm. Maybe if one of the advertising executives went there it would be bad because they could take some of their clients with them, but no client is going to go with Ruth.

"So, I'm here in the building to collect my things, but I suppose you're wondering why I'm here, as in here in your office," Ruth says after a moment.

I nod. I'm more than a little bit curious about that. It's not like I'm one of the people she would want to say goodbye to or exchange details with or anything.

"Well, I just wanted to say that there's no hard feelings from my end," Ruth says.

I should think there bloody well isn't. God, she has some nerve, and even now, she can get under my skin with it so easily. Breathe, I tell myself. She's the one who did something bad not me. But she's going now, and I decide to throw her a bone.

"Same here Ruth," I say. "No hard feelings. I get it that sometimes if you like someone, it can make you do crazy things. Good luck in your new job."

"No Serena, you misunderstand me," Ruth says. "I mean there's no hard feelings when it comes to Wyatt. He'll get sick of you. You know that right? You'll start to bore him. And when you do, I'll be waiting."

I laugh. I can't help it. The icy cold look Ruth gives me tells me that was definitely not the reaction from me that she was going for. Oops.

"I'm sorry," I say after a moment. "It's just that you've always been there waiting, and he's never once gotten that desperate." She visibly flinches but I'm not done yet. She had every chance to walk out of here with her head held high, but she chose not to take them and instead to go down this route. "You might be right about Wyatt and me though. Maybe one day he will get sick of me. But even if that happens, you are delusional if you think for one second that he'd come looking for you."

Ruth stands up.

"This isn't over," she says like she's a cartoon villain.

"Oh, but it is. And you lost," I say. "You lost your job. You lost your chance to leave with dignity. And most of all, you didn't get your man. Now go and enjoy life at Stoddard and Keel. Who knows, maybe there's someone there who you can stalk for a change."

She opens her mouth, but nothing comes out and she closes it again and storms to the door and pulls it open.

"Goodbye Ruth," I say with a wide smile.

I can't help but laugh and shake my head as she slams the

office door. I can't wait to tell Brook about this. She will absolutely love it.

* * *

"I still can't believe this is what you thought your party to celebrate you scoring your first client was going to be," Samantha says with a laugh, looking around the conference room.

It's a friendly laugh, like she's laughing with me rather than at me and I join her. It is comical when I think back to the party, the venue, the way people dressed to impress, and I thought it was going to be just like this. A few sausage rolls and canapes with warm champagne in the break room of the office. This party isn't even that lame. It's in the conference room so there is plenty of room for everyone rather than the break room where it would be rather cramped and while there is champagne circulating, it's not warm. The only real similarities are the sausage rolls being offered, and everyone loves a good sausage roll so I can forgive that one.

This time, Wyatt decided to do the party here. He said that landing Bellisario's was too big of an achievement for the company to just let it go without any celebrations at all, but because it wasn't a new associate involved with it, there was no guest of honor, so it seemed a bit over the top doing the whole party thing like he did for the associates when they landed their first clients. Generally speaking, he doesn't throw a party every time someone lands a client. Only new associates getting their first one, or something as huge as Bellisario's.

To be honest, as much as I enjoyed my party, I kind of prefer the more chilled out vibe of this one. My party felt like an event that people were using to mingle and impress, where this one feels like colleagues celebrating together. It started at five and it is likely to be over at seven, which I'm also pleased about, because it means that I can show my face, be sociable, and still have time to spend time with Wyatt this evening. Alone time rather than more hiding our relationship time.

CHAPTER 43

Serena

I move about the room talking to people. I answer a million questions about being in Rome and what it's like and what Mr Bellisario is like, and what our hotel was like, all of which are topics I try to answer the questions I get asked on as best as I can. Of course, there's the fourth topic too – the elephant in the room so to speak – Ruth and what happened to get her fired while we were in Italy. Whenever that one comes up, I just dodge it and say I don't really know and it's none of my business anyway. That puts everyone except the biggest gossips to shame. Most of them see themselves in the bit where I say it's not my business because it's also not theirs, but the real gossip seekers just laugh and say it doesn't matter whose business it is, they need to know all about it. I tell them I haven't been here long enough to be privy to that kind of information and they just believe me, assuming that Wyatt asked me to leave the room while he spoke to Ruth. I think if he hadn't yelled at me, he would have, but that was my vindication, getting to see firsthand what really happened to that slide.

Finally, people start to drift off and I decide to be one of them. As long as I'm not the first to go, I don't feel like I'm drawing attention to myself or being unsociable. I go around and say my goodbyes. When I say goodbye to Wyatt, he smiles at me and then he looks at his watch and does a show of not realizing the time.

"If you can give me two minutes to run back to my office and grab my things, I'll give you a ride home," he says. "I didn't realize the time."

"Ok, thank you," I say all sweetness and light like he isn't coming back to my place to fuck my brains out. "I'll wait at the elevators."

I don't have to wait long before Wyatt joins me, and we go down to the lobby together and then out into the parking lot and into his car. He starts the engine and pulls out and heads towards my place.

"I don't know what it is about champagne, but it always makes me horny," I say after a moment.

Wyatt laughs and accelerates slightly.

"You are always horny," he says.

"Is that a problem?" I ask, knowing it isn't or he wouldn't have accelerated.

"No," he says quickly. "In fact, it's the very opposite of a problem. What would that be?"

"A solution?" I suggest.

"Hmm that doesn't really work does it. Let's just stick with it not being a problem in any way, shape, or form," Wyatt says. "And know now if that ever changes, I will be bulk buying champagne and leaving it all around my apartment, your house and the office, just to be sure you have some."

I laugh and Wyatt laughs with me.

"I don't think it will come to that, but just so you know, if you do decide to do that, I'm partial to strawberries with my champagne," I say, still laughing.

"Oh, you're pushing your luck now," Wyatt says. "Champagne and strawberries. How frivolous."

We get to my place, and we get out of the car and head inside. We practically run up the garden path to my house. We reach the front door and I fumble my keys out of my purse and unlock the front door. I move aside and let Wyatt in first and then I follow and kick the front door closed behind us. I go to lock the door, but I drop my bunch of keys. I think about getting them, but Wyatt is pulling me towards him, and he is so much more appealing than my keys. Fuck it. I can lock the door later. It's not like I live somewhere dangerous.

I melt into Wyatt's arms and into his kiss as he walks me into the living room, his mouth not leaving mine. As we reach the living room, I push his jacket off his shoulders, and he unwraps his arms from around me just long enough to take the jacket off and throw it onto the couch. We are still joined at the mouth, but Wyatt pulls away quickly to whip his tie over his head and then our mouths come back together in a desperate, hungry kiss.

I start unbuttoning Wyatt's shirt and when it's all open I run my hands over his belly and chest, loving the feel of the solidness beneath his skin. I moan into his mouth in appreciation of Wyatt's hot body. I run my hands down his sides and then up and down his back, caressing his skin and running my nails lightly over it, something that I know turns him on so much.

My doorbell buzzes at that point and Wyatt and I both jump. Our kiss comes apart as we laugh at our own jumpiness.

"Are you not going to answer it?" Wyatt asks.

I shake my head.

"No. I'm not expecting anyone. It'll be someone trying to

sell me shit or have me sign their petition or something equally annoying," I say. "Now. Where were we?"

Wyatt leans in to kiss me again.

"Ah yes. Right there," I say and then I can't say anything else because my tongue is otherwise engaged with Wyatt's tongue.

I reach down and open his trousers and that's when the front door opens, and my dad walks in. I know it's him a second before he's in the room because he's already lecturing me about my front door being unlocked.

Fuck. The one time I don't lock the front door. And the one time I ignore the doorbell instead of feeling rude and opening the door and then having to try and politely get rid of whoever is there trying to sell me something.

Wyatt and I jump apart like we are suddenly repelled by each other, but it's far too late for my dad to think anything is happening here other than what was happening – something I very much didn't want him to know. With Wyatt's shirt open, his hands desperately fastening his trousers, and my hair all over the place and the redness around my lips, you would have to be blind not to see what was right there in front of you.

I realize my dad's lecture kind of stopped when he saw what was going on and I dare to glance at him. I feel like time has stopped but really it hasn't, and I see my dad running at Wyatt.

"Dad. Stop," I say, but he doesn't take any notice of me.

"You bastard. She was meant to be safe with you," my dad roars at Wyatt.

"She is safe with me," Wyatt says as he ducks back to avoid my dad's swinging fists.

I hate this. My dad and my partner fighting like this can't end well. One of them will end up hurt and I don't want either of them to be hurt, especially not when they are fighting about me. I move closer to them and get between them and then I put a palm on each of their chests and push them apart.

"Enough," I shout, trying to stop the fight before it really gets going.

I know I'm not strong enough to really hold them apart, so the fact they don't go for each other again shows that neither of them wants me to end up in the crossfire and I will use that to my advantage if it kicks off again.

"I think you should leave," my dad says to Wyatt.

"No," I say. "He's not going anywhere."

My dad opens his mouth to argue with me and I shake my head. I sigh and go on.

"Look this isn't the way I wanted you to find out about this, but it's not some random fling, Dad. I ... I am in love with Wyatt. He's the one, and I want to be with him forever," I say.

Wyatt takes my hand in his and squeezes it gently. For a second, I see my dad's anger flare up but then it seems to subside again.

"It's true Martin," Wyatt says. "Honestly. I feel the same way about her. I love her so much and I would never hurt her. You have to believe that."

For a moment, no one says anything, and it occurs to me that that's the first time Wyatt and I have told each other that we love each other. It really wasn't the way I expected it to be, but I'm just happy to hear that my feelings aren't one sided.

My dad breaks the spell and moves, sitting down heavily in the middle of the couch. He shakes his head and then looks at Wyatt and then at me and then he shakes his head again.

"This isn't real. It can't be. My little girl ..." he says.

I go and sit down beside him and put my hand on his arm.

"I know in your eyes I will always be your little girl, but I'm a grown woman Dad," I say. "And I can make my own decisions about who I do or don't date. I know you're not going to like it, but can you at least accept it? Please?"

It's important to me that my dad at least tries to get on board with my relationship with Wyatt. He's my only parent and I don't want to lose him as well.

"Dad?" I prompt after a moment.

He sighs and rubs his hands over his face.

"I apologize for going to hit you," he says to Wyatt.

"No worries," Wyatt said. "I probably would have reacted the same myself with the shock of finding out like that."

"I don't know if I will ever be fully ok with this, but I promise I will try to be," he says to me. He sighs again. "I mean I guess if you're going to grow up and be with someone, it may as well be Wyatt than some stranger. At least I know that he will treat you right."

"Thank you," I say. "For trying I mean. It means a lot to me."

My dad puts his arm around my shoulders and gives me a squeeze and then he focuses on Wyatt again.

"I'm going to go now. And when I do, you're going to fasten that shirt, and you're not going to touch my daughter again until you make an honest woman of her. Do you hear me?" he says.

"Loud and clear," Wyatt says.

"And?" my dad presses him.

"And I won't touch her until I make an honest woman of her," Wyatt says.

"I expect you to honor that as well young lady," my dad says to me and then he stands up. "Right, I'll leave you two to it. Not to that. Oh hell, you know what I mean."

I walk him to the door of the house and when he steps out into the garden, I momentarily follow him.

"I know this is going to be hard for you," I say. I can feel tears burning my eyes. "But please try. I ... I can't bear the thought of losing you."

He pulls me into a tight hug.

"You will never lose me girl, you hear me," he says gruffly and then he releases me. "I'll make my peace with you two. Now go on, before you have your old man all emotional."

I laugh through the blur of tears, and then I go back inside. I scoop my keys up off the floor, making sure to lock my front door this time – the phrase too little too late comes to mind, but it's done now, and I won't make that mistake again. I hang my keys on the little hook at the end of my coat hooks and I go back to the living room, and I find Wyatt on his cell phone. I sit down and wait until he is finished on his call. He ends the call not much later and smiles at me.

"That was your Uncle Craig," he says. "I couldn't bear the idea of your dad telling him about us before I got the chance to."

"Is he pissed off?" I ask.

Wyatt smiles and shakes his head.

"No. His exact words were 'well duh it took you two long enough'," Wyatt says.

"I guess we aren't as subtle as we think we are," I say.

"I don't know. I think Craig knows me way better than anyone else and you and him are close too. I think it would take some doing to fool Craig for too long," Wyatt says.

"Yeah true," I say. "Oh, and by the way, now you've made that promise to my dad, I hate to rush things, but we'd better hurry up and get married."

"Why? Are you that horny for me already?" Wyatt says with a laugh.

"I mean yes," I say. "But that's not why. I'm kind of already pregnant."

I wait to see how Wyatt will react. For a second, he just

stands there, but then his face lights up in a huge smile and he pulls me to my feet and hugs me tightly and then we kiss and any promise to my dad goes quickly out of the window. Sorry Dad, I think to myself. But this already feels like Wyatt has made an honest woman out of me as my dad put it, because I know that this is forever. I don't need a piece of paper to tell me that much.

Epilogue
SERENA

Eighteen Months Later

S o, we didn't quite manage the wedding. But we did get engaged. And we are going to get married, but we have decided we want to wait until Ophelia, our daughter, is old enough to be a part of it and to remember it too. My dad took it all quite well considering how he found out about us and then considering we broke our word to him.

I really think it helped with him accepting us when Ophelia came along and my dad did what we all did – he took one look at those chubby cheeks and those large blue eyes, and he fell in love with her, and the feeling was mutual. Even now on her first birthday with friends and family around, a face painter, a bouncy castle and games, Ophelia only wants her grandad.

Wyatt comes up behind me and sees me watching Ophelia sitting on my dad's lap. He's talking away to her and whatever he is saying, it's making her laugh her sweet little laugh. Wyatt wraps his arms around my waist and rests his chin on my shoulder for a moment.

"She's so beautiful, just like her mom," he says.

He releases me and stands beside me, and I smile up at him. He leans down and kisses me, and I kiss him back. We pull apart and smile at each other and I glance back at Ophelia. My dad is looking right at me, and I catch his eye and instead of looking angry like he would have this time last year at Wyatt and me kissing, or even uncomfortable, like he has for the last few months, he looks happy for me. For us. And in that moment, I feel happy and content and like the luckiest girl in the world because I know now that we will be ok.

Me, Wyatt, Ophelia, and all of our extended family. We are all going to be just fine together.

THE END

Coming Soon - Sample Chapter

CONFESSING TO THE CEO

Chapter 1
Scarlett

As a principle, I don't run.

For anyone or anything.

But the moment Sophie called with that strain of pain in her barely audible voice, I found myself running through the city, and hailing down taxis to get to her.

"He's gone, Scar," she whispered in awed voice. "I think he's really gone. Please come over. I'm in Queens. Flushing Meadows Corona park."

I knew she was scheduled to meet her wedding planner and caterer at an event this evening, along with her fiancé Jerald. So, the fact that this was happening was alarming, to say the least. As I rushed to her, I realized I couldn't recall the last time I'd seen her distraught, and I grew even more worried.

She'd never burden anyone with her pain unless it was

quite literally so intense everyone could feel it and asked her about it. The closer I got to her, the more anxious I became.

I spotted her sitting alone, her shoulders slumped, at a table in the big hall, facing the huge windows. The sun was already setting, and the view through the garden beyond was breathtaking.

"Sophie," I called, but she didn't hear me. She was so lost in her thoughts that even though my voice echoed through the nearly empty huge hall.

"Sophis," I called even louder, a touch of panic in my voice.

She turned then, and I stopped in my tracks.

My God, she looked devastated. Her face was pale and pinched, and her eyes were red and swollen. Of course, I knew she'd had her doubts; I saw it once or twice in her eyes when they'd argued, but she had never shared them or complained.

"Bastard," I muttered, as I squatted in front of her and held the sides of her arms.

She shook her head. "Don't blame him. He's having a hard time. He's just lost his mom. I understand, I do, it's really hard for him. They were so close..."

She could say whatever she wanted, but as I watched my twin, the person I loved most in the world, look so dejected and sit in front of me, as though everything she was had been sucked out of her, I couldn't help but feel hurt and furious at the same time.

Somehow, I managed to compose myself and rein in my emotions so that I could show up for her as she needed, not as I wanted.

"What happened?" I asked.

She managed to trembling smile. "You had your presentation today, right? How was it?"

"Are you kidding me?" asked incredulously. "You're talking about that now?"

She wiped away tears from the corners of her eye to prevent them from falling. "I don't want to talk about it yet. I don't know how to even get up from this chair. I don't know how to survive the next second. So I've just been sitting here..."

"Did he give you a reason?" I asked.

She inhaled deeply and released it slowly. "He did, but it made no sense. I mean... it did, but it's not enough. I can't accept it. We've been together too long."

She shook her head. "I love him and I hate him at the same time."

My brows furrowed at this. I truly didn't want to rush her. I just wanted to be here to listen, so she could speak as slowly as she wanted. However, I truly wanted to get something out of the way.

"He didn't cheat on you, right?"

She lifted her gaze to look at me blankly. "I don't know."

My face immediately darkened. "Do you suspect it?"

"I have no clue," she said. "But I don't think so. I just think he's a bit sad and lost. He's lost the only parent he had."

She paused again.

"To be honest, I'm not completely surprised. The signs have been there for the last seven months. I was just hoping it would pass. Then we got engaged, and I was sure that all was well, but now..."

"He was supposed to meet me here, but he called and said he needed time away. From me... from everything. To think, to understand, to digest the loss, because since then, he hasn't been able to see anything clearly without his grief tainting it. Even me."

"Okay, that's not so bad. He just needs time, then. I can understand that," I consoled.

She nodded. "I do as well, but it doesn't change the fact that I've been abandoned mere weeks before our wedding. The invitations have gone out, I've been with him for nearly seven years of my life. Was all of that just a waste?"

More tears escaped from the corners of her eyes.

"It can't just have been a waste. I love him with my whole heart. I still..." she stopped herself. "God, I feel so pathetic. I really can't believe this."

"Did he give any indications that he'll come back?" I asked, and she let out a dark scoff.

"He didn't give any indication of anything whatsoever, the freaking asshole."

A smile tugged at the corners of my lips, however. It was just so funny to see her curse. She almost never did. She was the complete opposite of me, and I'd always teased her for it.

"What did you say to him?" I asked.

She went silent for a few seconds. "What could I say?"

"Maybe what he needed... " I paused. "Maybe what he needs is someone to talk some sense into him. Maybe you've coddled him a bit too much, and so he's just wallowed and completely rotted in his grief... no offense."

"So you're saying this is my fault?"

I sighed. "You know that's not what I'm saying."

"So what are you saying?"

"He's always loved you because of your temperament. He loves how calm and considerate you are, but maybe during this time in his life, that's not what he needs. Maybe he needs someone to be like a bucket of ice-cold water dumped over his obtuse head. Maybe that's what he needs to see clearly."

She smiled a little, and it was such a relieve that I almost didn't know how to contain myself.

"I mean it though," I said.

She nodded. "I know what you mean, and I tried that,

trust me. It didn't work. Nothing worked. He just... he just seems broken and destroyed, and once again, I'm not a monster. I do understand, and this is the most frustrating part. Now, I'm almost kind of wishing he cheated on me so that I'd have a very valid reason to vent and scream. As it is the slow loss is just so quiet and deep and excruciating. There were no fights, no big blowouts... those at least, could be addressed and resolved, but this is just so quietly insidious. A simple phone call to inform me that he needs to be away from me, leaving me to do whatever I want as a result."

"So you didn't curse him out at all?" I asked, shocked. Boy, I would have turned the air blue if someone had pulled that on me so near my wedding.

"Not this time, but I did two weeks back," she replied. "We had a fight a little while about the way he didn't seem to care about our wedding." Her brow creased. 'Do you think that was the reason why he broke things off today."

I was surprised to hear this. "You? You lost it with him?"

"Yeah," she replied. "He... he has a six-figure bakery. I couldn't wrap my head around the fact that despite this, he didn't care who would handle our cake or pastries. I showed him some photos, and he was so disinterested. He just wanted me to contract it out to whoever."

"What?" I frowned.

"Sophie, I love you, and I'm sorry for saying this, but are you sure his grief is what has him acting like a complete tool or he's just acting like it for no reason?"

She was silent for a while, then she shrugged. "I really don't know. That's what's killing me in all of this. I really don't know. I always felt like I understood him deeply, like we were on the same wavelength but... now he feels even more distant to me than a stranger."

Maybe this was for the best, then, I thought, but I didn't

dare say it out loud. She looked at me then as though she could read what I was thinking – this had been the case numerous times in the past.

"What?" I asked.

"I want to still try... I can't give up easily."

I immediately started to shut this down, but then once again held back. She kept staring at me.

"What?" I frowned.

"I know what you're thinking."

I didn't deny this possibility.

"Okay," I replied, and her face weakened as though she was about to cry again.

"Sophie, come on."

She reached forward and hit my shoulder. "I need you to be on my side right now."

"That's why I'm not saying anything," I replied.

"So, do you think I should?"

"Should you what?" I asked, hoping that she would quickly abandon this horrendous notion.

"Do you think I should give up?"

"He wants you to," I replied, and tears filled her eyes again. I leaned forward then and pulled her into my arms.

"You know what Mom always used to say," I said. "Time resolves all problems so..."

"You think I should give it time."

I was hesitant to say this as well, so she leaned away to look at me.

"You never liked him."

"It's not just him I don't like," I said.

She sighed.

"He's okay, but you, I love, so I say, take the time off and let's see how you feel."

She pulled away from me. "I can't take the time off right now."

"Why not?"

She picked up her purse, and we began to leave. "Things are hellish at work, and my boss doesn't understand what excuses are. I can't leave."

"What do you mean your boss doesn't understand what excuses are?"

She shrugged in response, and we walked on to catch a taxi. One stopped almost as soon as we reached the stand. Inside she turned to me.

"What?" I asked.

She narrowed her gaze at me but didn't say a word. Then she shook her head and looked away.

I wondered what gears were turning in her head, but knowing her, I knew she primarily wouldn't spit it out until she had thought it through properly.

"We still look alike, right?" she asked out of the blue, and the question startled me.

"What?"

"I asked, we're still identical, right? Indistinguishable."

"I have no idea," I said, "but we haven't been mistaken for one another for a long time."

"That's because your style changed in college. Your makeup is bolder, your hair's a bob, your outfit..."

I grinned. "You mean I'm hot. Yeah, I get it."

She smiled, but her gaze began to rove over my face in earnest.

"What are you thinking?" I asked worriedly.

"You know what I'm thinking."

My eyebrows nearly shot up to my hairline, and I began to shake my head. "No... no... no..."

"Oh please, Scarlett. Can you?"

I watched her. "You're serious?"

"Why not? We've done it so many times."

"That was when we were kids," I stated, still shaking my head.

"No, we did it in college and during your internship, at that first company you worked for. I did it because you needed my help. I did it for you. Will you do it for me?"

I kept staring at her, then I looked away.

I heard her sigh. "It's okay if you don't want to do it? We haven't been too close these past few years, have we? Because I instead invested all my time with that jerk."

"We're twins," I said softly. "Even though we drift apart sometimes, we'll always have each other and no one else."

She smiled then and leaned against me, resting her head on my shoulder. She remained silent for a few blocks further, and then she brought it up once again.

"So..." she said. "Do you think you can pull it off?"

I considered her request. It felt too strange to be her after all these years. We were not kids or in college anymore.

"Are you able to leave your current job?"

"I always can," I replied. "That's one of the benefits of going the freelance route."

"When was your contract due to end?" she asked.

"I still have a month and a half left," I replied.

"Oh..." she said, her voice forlorn.

"Don't worry," I told her. "It's not hard for me to find another place. I'll help you out. Just tell me that your current workload is not much. What do I have to deal with this coming week?"

She smiled at her and told a blatant lie. "Not much at all."

I narrowed my gaze at her and she looked away quickly.

Oh my God! I knew that look. It was going to be a mad week.

"Whatever it is, I'll handle it. But wait, where is your company located? In Manhattan?"

She bit her bottom lip. "Yes."

I sucked in a breath through my teeth.

"A bit too far from Soho?"

"A bit," I replied.

"I can pay for your taxi for the week?" she suggested.

"You don't have to do that."

"It's no trouble, I know you hate the subway, plus Montgomery pays quite handsomely, so it's not a problem."

"Montgomery?" I asked, and she nodded.

"My boss. His name is Lucien. Montgomery is his surname."

"Ah, so that's where the company name Montgomery Holdings comes from?"

"Yeah," she replied.

"And he's filthy rich, right?"

"Net worth is just under two billion."

"Wow. How ancient is he?"

"Thirty-two years old," she replied.

My mouth nearly fell open. "What?"

"Young, huh?"

I nodded. "Way too young. I was hoping he was an elderly boss that could barely see. Then it would be most likely that we could get away with this."

She thought about this, parted her lips, but closed them back.

"What?" I asked.

"He acts quite aloof, like he doesn't know anything, but sometimes I'm able to listen to his conversations, and I'm actually amazed by how much he knows. About the company, about everything. Like we're situated on various floors, and sometimes I hear what is going on just by listening to him. I low-key think there's a spy somewhere in the office that silently feeds him information; otherwise, I have no clue how he literally knows everything happening at a given time."

"So he's nosy?" I asked.

"Not nosy but vigilant, I think is the appropriate word. His day has to be completely organized, and he has a huge client he's planning on signing this week," she said, stopping at the realization of the magnitude of her work either.

"Wow," she said to herself as she thought. "This is truly a bad time to leave. I'll wait for the week to run out, maybe some other -"

Suddenly her phone began to ring, so she got up and pulled the phone out of her pocket. She, however, didn't respond. Instead, she stared at it until I was forced to check who it was. Montgomery was clearly written as the caller.

"Is that him?" I asked.

"Yeah," she said, and then to my surprise, she passed the phone over to me.

"What?"

"Answer it," she said. "Our voices are similar, but I think my pitch is slower than yours. Let's see, first of all, if he'll notice the difference."

I stared at the phone as it continued to ring, all the while she urged it towards me.

"Answer it," she said, but I hesitated. Eventually, I sighed, but just as I accepted it, it disconnected.

"I started to hand it over, but she stopped me. "He'll call back. He wouldn't be calling if it wasn't important. That's good, at least he doesn't disturb you."

"Oh no, he does. He doesn't call me late because he

doesn't have to. I'll probably be in the office working late with him."

"Oh no," I wrinkled my nose. "You have to work late a lot?"

"Usually, but the bonuses are insane, plus lately I've been glad to be anywhere but home," I stared at her and couldn't help but feel saddened by her words.

"We've really not been as close as we should be? I should know this?"

"We talk a lot, just not about these things, plus I didn't exactly want to tell you about Jerald either."

"You're right," I nodded, "It's all your fault."

She smiled, and just then the phone began to ring again.

"Speaker," she said. "Try it out."

I nodded and responded.

"Sophie, where's the shares division proposal?" came the cold, quiet voice.

For a moment, I was a bit startled as I listened to him because I had expected a boisterous tone. However, he sounded so calm like the undulating surface of the ocean.

"Hello?" he called again.

I turned to look at Sophie, who was thinking.

Eventually she figured it out and raised her hand. "It's on my desktop," she whispered.

"Sophie!" he called again, and though his tone wasn't loud, I could still feel the annoyance in his tone.

"Oh, sorry," I replied.

Sophie mouthed the next set of instructions to me. "Sorry, Sir."

"What?" I mouthed back.

"Sir," she whispered fiercely, and my frown deepened even further.

"Sophie?" he reminded again, and she nudged me.

255

"Sorry, Sir, it's on my desktop."

He went silent briefly. "You didn't print it out? You said you'd leave the documents on my desk."

I watched the worry flash across Sophie's face. Then she began to nod, and my attention focused on her lips. "I did, Sir, but I think I left that one out."

Once again, he went silent.

"I expected him to hang up then or scold her and get someone else to do what he wanted, but he dished out new instructions over the phone.

"I need those documents now," he said.

I frowned again, before I could tell him to go bother himself, in other more colorful words, Sophie nodded vigorously at me while whispering, "I'll be there in a little while."

I was forced to repeat the words, and afterward, I set the cell phone down.

"You'll be there in a little while?"

"I'm his personal assistant," she told me. "He has others, but I'm the only one with complete access to him. Others are restricted in one way or another, and I'm the only one with a hefty salary and additional bonuses."

I still wasn't convinced, however, she wasn't interested in trying to convince me. "I want to build a long-term career there; you don't, so—"

"I know, jeez, don't rub it in."

"So, will you go?"

"Wait, what?" I asked, taken aback.

"It's just to give him some documents, let's do this as a test run."

"But... we look so different," I pointed out.

She assessed my appearance and nodded. "Yes, we do, but that's quite easily fixed."

I couldn't help but admit that I was curious about her boss.

"He doesn't know you have an identical twin, does he?" I asked.

"Nope. He knows almost nothing about me," she replied. Then she stopped herself. "Wait, as I said earlier, he always seems to know more than he lets on. So maybe he does know, hence the need for a test. So if he asks who you are when you go there now, you can make up something like I'm on my way, and if he doesn't ask, then the coast is clear."

"And my hair?" I asked. "How do I explain why I suddenly have a bob rather than a bun and different clothes for that matter?"

She looked at me. "Don't worry about that. He wouldn't notice if you went in with a bikini."

"As if," I scoffed

"I've been working directly with him for over three years, and there hasn't even been a tense moment between us."

"Is he gay?" I asked.

She smiled. "Absolutely not."

"What makes you so sure?"

"You'll see," she said, with a secret smile.

"On second thought, and just to be safe, I'm not looking to lose my job. Let's exchange clothes. We can explain away the haircut, but clothes for sure will be much harder."

I perused her dress shirt, buttoned down almost to the collar, her pencil skirt, and flats.

She smiled again. "You look absolutely disgusted."

"Why do you dress like that?" I asked "You look like Aunt Theresa, only a hundred pounds lighter. Maybe this is why there hasn't been any tension."

"And I would like extremely keen for it to remain that way." She gave me a look.

I brushed her concern away. "Don't worry, I wouldn't dream of seducing your boss."

Pre-order the book here:

Confessing to the CEO

About the Author

Thank you so much for reading!
If you have enjoyed the book and would like to leave a
precious review for me, please kindly do so here:

Strictly Business

Please click on the link below to receive info about my latest
releases and giveaways.
<u>NEVER MISS A THING</u>

Or
come say 'hello' here:

Also by Iona Rose

Printed in Great Britain
by Amazon

35717401R00153